Clara Jessup Bloomfield

Gondaline's Lesson - The Warden's Tale

Stories for Children and Other Poems

Clara Jessup Bloomfield

Gondaline's Lesson - The Warden's Tale
Stories for Children and Other Poems

ISBN/EAN: 9783744716000

Printed in Europe, USA, Canada, Australia, Japan

Cover: Foto ©Andreas Hilbeck / pixelio.de

More available books at **www.hansebooks.com**

GONDALINE'S LESSON
THE WARDEN'S TALE
STORIES FOR CHILDREN

AND OTHER POEMS

BY

MRS BLOOMFIELD MOORE

'Disdain us not, O kindly heart of man !
Us unregarded poets of the earth,
The feeble songsters singing as we can
Our eager melodies of little worth'

LONDON
C. KEGAN PAUL & CO., 1 PATERNOSTER SQUARE
1881

	PAGE
At Home, May 1864	177
Widowed	178
Our Hero	181

THE SEASONS.

An April Day	185
A Day in Midsummer	187
Autumn Scenes	190
Winter	192

SONNETS.

I. Morning	197
II. Noon	198
III. Night	199

ERAS IN LIFE.

Forebodings	203
Thorns and Arrows	204
My Gethsemane	207
'O God, Be Pitiful'	209
'Be Brave'	211
Submission	212
Evil and Good	214
Wrecked	216
Dead Hopes	218
Waiting	220
Memorial	222
The Ministering Spirit	224

MISCELLANEOUS.

POEMS.

GONDALINE'S LESSON.

Faust.—Nun gut, wer bist du denn?
Meph.—Ein Theil von jener Kraft die stets das Böse will, und stets das Gute schafft.—GOETHE.

[*Faust.*—Well, good! who art thou then?
Meph.—A part of that power that always wants evil, but always creates good.]

THE Prince of Evil from his lurid home
    Sent to our world, on mission fraught with ill,
An angel wondrous fair to look upon,
    A Lucifer in point of cunning skill.

Landing on earth, the angel walked with men;
    They knew him not as other than their kin:
And one, ruling as lord in wide domain,
    Threw open doors and took the angel in.

With form like Juno's and a heart of gold,
    Fairer than Helen, was his beauteous queen:
Gracious as goddess stooping down to man
    The stranger guest was met by Gondaline.

The angel held aloof, nor sought to win
  One smile other than those she freely gave ;
Serene his front as theirs who never sin,
  Serene his eyes as theirs who live to save.

The days passed on, and like a sister kind
  Grew day by day the fair and gracious queen ;
The weeks passed by, and like a sister fond
  More gracious grew the lovely Gondaline.

When one full month had folded happy days,
  As the ripe wheat folds close within its core
The hoarded sweetness of the sun's warm rays
  When drooping sheaves are bound for garnered
    store,

The angel ~~guest~~ feigned that he must depart—
  Deep sadness in his eyes and in his mien,
Trembled his voice whene'er he spoke, ~~unto~~
  The trustful, gentle, gracious Gondaline.

' Why wilt thou leave us ?' the fair woman asked,
  And none were near to hear the answer given.
' I go,' he said, ' because I dare not stay :
  I am as one shut out from hopes of heaven.'

'And why is this?'   Her eyes were raised to his.
  'Some secret meaning in your words are hid.'
'You say aright : I dare not plainer speak
  Unless by your sweet lips mine own are bid.'

                    my friend,
'Tell me thy grief,' ~~she said~~, 'and I will pray
  Unto our Lord to lift the heavy load.'
He shuddered as she spoke, and turned away
  As one who finds a barrier on his road.

'Fear not.   I will thy secret guard
  As if it were a secret of my own.
I would that I could help thee on thy way—
  Burdens are lightened when not borne alone.'

                              fair one,
'Ah, thou couldst help me if thou wouldst, ~~he said~~;
  But in dark ways thy feet have never trod,
And thou wouldst fear to go where I must walk !'
  'Nothing I fear save conscience and my God !'

Again he quailed and cowered at the word ;
  Then raised his eyes, and met her questioning
    gaze :
Hers were as virginal as maiden's are ;
          unholy
  His with ~~dark~~ passions were ablaze.

' I am no coward,' said, *were the words she* she unto him,

'And in those ways, howe'er so dark they be,

I should not fear, nor from them turn aside,

If in them I could be of use to thee.'

Nearer she drew, and took his hand in hers,

Nor did she fear when close he held her own ;

Nearer he drew, and bent his face to hers,

Saying some words in low and eager tone.

She felt his gaze as snow feels morning sun,

While her lips moved in earnest, pleading prayer :

' Dear Lord, give me this precious soul to save !

Help him, whate'er it is, his cross to bear !'

Once more he shrank, as if a thing of naught ;

Once more their eyes were turned in steadfast

gaze :

It was as if some power passed from her,

Drawing him from the evil of his ways.

' I would not harm thee if I could,' he said :

' I go to tell my master I have seen

A spirit pure as heaven's angels are,

In thy chaste eyes, thou wondrous Gondaline.

' I go to tell him that I cannot fill

   The harmful mission which his mandate sent :

I would not wrong thee, if I could, ~~he said~~ *dear one* ,

   While on him still her questioning eyes were bent.

' How couldst thou wrong me ?' she the answer
     made.

  ' I ~~seek~~ *with* to do thee good ; thou couldst not do me
    ill !

All things together work for weal, we know,

   To those who work for good and seek God's will

' Thy master hath no power, save God permits ;

   And He guards those who strive to do His will :

Go, tell thy master this, whose evil good may bring

   To thee, and me, God's purpose to fulfil.

' I know thee now—a minister of Sin !

   But thou a lesson unto me hast taught :

The soul of good may e'en in evil dwell,

   The soul of evil e'en in good be brought !'

LOVE'S FOUR SEASONS.

'Where love is, heaven is.'

BARBARA'S HISTORY.

I

WHAT time sad Winter's snows cold-sowed the
    earth,
And leaden skies hid heaven from our sight,
While wrangling winds wailed o'er their tortured
    birth
    Through short cold days and long cold hours of
    night,
Love planted in my heart his seeds of fire,
    Thrilling each vein with vibrant, strange delight,
Changing my pulses to electric wire,
    Though still his face was hidden from my sight.

II

What time the goddess of the Spring came down
    To bring her yearly offering of flowers,
And Earth threw off her icy veil and gown,
    Her bosom quickening in the sun-god's showers,

When virginal fields of pale forget-me-not
   Couched side by side with amorous clover lay,
Then walked I in those fields with Love, I wot,
   Still blindly trusting him to lead the way.

III

What time hot Summer's throbbing skies of blue
   Shone o'er these meadows where our steps had
     strayed,
And her warm breath, steeped in rich fragrance
     through,
   Filled with sweet languors all the hours we
     made,
I saw Love's face, and all my blood to flame
   He kindled with his asking eyes on mine ;
And I, divining what he wished to claim,
   Said in my heart, 'Already I am thine.'

IV

What time the purple grapes hung on the vine,
   And pregnant Earth was teeming with her fruit,
And men and maidens harvested the wine,
   Dancing at close to zittern and to lute :

Within Love's arms, close circling me around,
Languid with kisses which his warm lips rained,
I said, 'At last life's secret I have found,
At last my earthly paradise is gained.'

THE WARDEN'S TALE.

A Parable for the Age.

Oh, the little more, and how much it is,
And the little less, and what worlds away.
R. Browning.

I

I am warden of a garden—
Of a garden quaint and fair—
Seldom does the king, my master, .
Ever wish to wander there.

II

Little cares he for the blossoms
Or the fruits beside the wall;
In the centre blooms a rose tree,
And the roses he claims all.

III

But one day there came a pilgrim,
Lofty air yet winning mien,
And he asked a tiny flower
Pale as is the moonlight's sheen.

IV

So I plucked and gave it to him,
　And he wore it on his breast
As we walked along the garden,
　Pausing here and there to rest.

V

Day by day returned this pilgrim;
　As we paced the shaded aisles
Friendlier grew his words of greeting,
　Tenderer his friendly smiles.

VI

And we often gathered flowers—
　Spotless lilies, pansies cold
As the purple in the heavens
　When it borders twilight's gold.

VII

But one day our footsteps straying
　To the garden's centre came,
Where the roses on the branches
　Bloomed with tropic hearts of flame.

VIII

Then with lips so sweet and tender,
  And with eyes more tender still,
'Give me but one rose,' he whispered,
  'And then ask whate'er you will.'

IX

How could I the rose refuse him,
  If his eyes my heart could melt?
So I stretched my hand to reach it,
  When a piercing thorn I felt.

X

'Ah! 'tis not my rose to give you!'
  With an aching heart I spake,
In the pain of that refusing
  Which I longed to have him take.

XI

' 'Tis but one rose that I asked for,'
  Straight he said, in grieved surprise ;
'When your master counts so many,
  Bloom they only for his eyes ?'

XII

'Take the violets, take the pansies,
　　Take the lilies, if you will,
But unworthy I for warden
　　If no trust I shall fulfil.

XIII

'And this rose bush, he has told me,
　　Must be left for him alone ;
So I cannot give his roses,
　　Though they are so thickly blown.'

XIV

'Give me one ; he will not miss it
　　Though he count them o'er and o'er—
Only one ; 'tis all I ask for,
　　And I ne'er will ask for more.

XV

'Give it, warden ; lips refusing
　　Wear not grace as when they yield ;
And I know the king, thy master,
　　Gathers in another field.'

XVI

Then I wavered.   In that moment
  He knew not the half my pain
As I answered, ' Reach and take it,
  For you shall not plead in vain.'

XVII

So, with eager hand approaching,
  He stooped low to pick the rose,
When a serpent, coiled beneath it,
  Did his fiery eyes disclose.

XVIII

Then I, shivering, started forward,
  All my heart with anguish torn :
' Leave the roses for the lilies ;
  They have neither sting nor thorn.'

XIX

But he drew me close beside him,
  And he whispered in my ear
Words that I, another's warden,
  Might not, ought not, dared not, hear.

XX

How I wrung my hands in sorrow,
　How my heart ached with despair,
How I prayed to God to help me,
　How He heard my frantic prayer,

XXI

Is a tale that ne'er was spoken;
　But the pilgrim since that day
Has not sought my master's roses,
　Has not even passed this way.

XXII

Now to other wardens say I—
　For I've won the right to speak
By the anguish of my spirit
　And the pallor of my cheek—

XXIII

King or prince, or who he may be
　That to thee doth trust confide,
Leave no pilgrim in the precincts,
　At his will to wander wide.

XXIV

Pick no pansies, no, nor lilies,
    To adorn another's breast
Than the one who is thy master,
    If thy conscience would have rest ;

XXV

For no pilgrim but will wander
    Where the owner's roses bloom,
When the lilies and the pansies
    Lose for him their faint perfume.

THE WEB OF LIFE.

My life, which was so straight and plain,
Has now become a tangled skein,
  Yet God still holds the thread ;
Weave as I may, His hand doth guide
The shuttle's course, however wide
  The chain in woof be wed.

One weary night, when years went by,
I plied my loom with tear and sigh,
  In grief unnamed, untold ;
But when at last the morning's light
Broke on my vision, pure and bright
  There gleamed a cloth of gold.

And now I never lose my trust,
Weave as I may—and weave I must—
  That God doth hold the thread ;
He guides my shuttle on its way,
He makes complete my task each day
  What more, then, can be said ?

THE MAIDEN'S FLOWER OMENS.

I

' If he bring me a rose, a briar rose,
   To place in my braided hair,
I shall know there are thorns in life for me
   And many a wearying care.

If he bring me a lily pure and pale
   And lay it upon my breast,
I shall know that my life will be of peace,
   As a bird in its mother's nest.

If he bring me pansies purple and gold
   And clasp them within my hand,
I shall know that rare treasures I will glean
   From many a distant land.

' If he bring me orange blossoms sweet,
   With their clinging buds beside,
I shall know that before the year is out
   I will surely be his bride.

' If he bring me blue forget-me-nots,
  As blue as the summer sky,
I shall know I will never falsehood see
  In the blue of his bonnie eye.

' If he bring me poppies red as the coals
  That glow in the blacksmith's fire,
I shall know like the coals his love will die
  In the ashes of his desire.

If he bring me soft carnation pinks
  Whose sweetness fills the air,
~~In a wreath as children wear,~~
I shall know it is but fancy for me,
  That with others I must share.

' If he bring me snowdrops waxen white
  That droop with their own weight low,
I will know, alas ! when the winter comes
  I shall sleep beneath the snow.'

II

Nor snowdrops white, nor pinks, nor blossoms pale,
  Were given to the maiden fair ;
Nor poppies red, nor blue forget-me-nots,
  Nor pansies yet, nor lilies rare ;

But laden down with roses came he then—
   Moss-roses, maiden-blush and white,
Burgundy roses crimson as the wine
   When crystal goblets flash the light;

Roses, like sea shells, with pink pearly tints,
   Roses with petals of rare yellow gold,
Roses as scarlet as a woman's lips
   When rain warm kisses all untold.

He flung them o'er her, laughing as they fell.
   No laughter rippled back to him :
' I hold an omen in these flowers,' she said,
   ' An omen for the future dim.

' Would you had brought me lilies in their stead,
   Or pansies with their hearts of gold,
Or dear forget-me-nots, that breathe of faith,
   Seeming some sacred trust to hold !

' But roses ! roses with their cruel thorns !
   Oft-times as false as fair are they,
Since canker-worms coil close within their hearts,
   Eating their fragrant life away.'

III

'Sad is the life where roses do not bloom ;
  And one forgives the thorns,' he said,
'When one has drunken of the rich perfume
  That regal roses always shed.

'I bring thee roses as unto a queen.
  If thou, sweet love, my queen wilt be,
Only the roses shalt thou have in life,
  And all the thorns shall be for me.'

She heard, and straight upon his breast she hid
  Her happy face, with blushes warm.
Her trusting heart believed the words he said ;
  He felt her answer in her clinging form.

No fairer bride e'er orange blossoms wore
  Than this sweet maid at chancel rail ;
No husband fond so kept the vows he made—
  Yet thorns with roses, reader, never fail.

BLOSSOMS AND THORNS.

UP to the courts of heaven fair
  A spirit sped one day ;
Released from earth, the spirit cried,
  ' Open the gate, I pray !'

An angel swung the golden door ;
  ' Where is thy cross ?' he said.
' Here is my crown ; I have no cross
  To offer in its stead.'

' No cross, no crown,' the answer made,
  And slowly turned the door ;
The pilgrim spirit bowed her head
  As one in sorrow sore.

' Dear Lord !' she cried, in her despair,
  ' Shut not the gate on me ;
Thorns are within the crown I wear
  Like those that piercèd Thee.'

Then quickly swung the gate again ;
  Our Lord Himself was there,
Whose ears are never, never closed
  Unto a sufferer's prayer.

' Woman, give Me your crown,' He said ;
  ' If martyr's thorns you wear,
You can pass in the golden gate
  With those who crosses bear.'

Then from her drooping head she took
  Its crown of blossoms bright ;
And, lo ! the piercing points within
  Revealed themselves to sight.

' Why hast thou worn this crown ? ' He asked ;
  ' Better a cross to bear.'
' I wore it, Lord, for love of him
  Who made and placed it there.'

' For love like this,' our Saviour said,
  ' Though to the creature given,
Thou hast done well to call on Me,
  For thou hast won thy heaven.'

THE MAGDALENE.

SUGGESTED BY A PAINTING OF A MAGDALENE.

Luke vii. 47.

BENEATH a sacred shrine she kneeled,
Her bosom's charms scarce half concealed,
'Tween flowing robe and hair revealed—

Hair of the hue of burnished gold,
Rippling along the dark blue fold
That wrapped a form of peerless mould.

' Oh, Christ ! ' she cried, ' here at Thy feet
I leave my tears, for tears are meet
For one who findeth sin so sweet !

' And yet, dear Lord, I love not sin,
And Thou, who readest hearts within,
See'st my soul doth oftenest win !

' But when his lips my own lips press
In royal bliss of tenderness,
Such as the angels cannot guess,

' Then sin no longer sin doth seem,
And wrapped as in a holy dream
I give my very self to him :

' I give, and weep I have no more
To give to him whom I adore,
And count my life of little store.

' If life for him I could but yield,
Nor priest to shrive, but unannealed,
I'd walk alone the shadowy field.

' To give him heaven I would dwell
Where, in rank groves of asphodel,
Tread spirits that from heaven fell.

' Forgive me, Lord, in that I love,
Nor close Thy courts to me above
If sinless in all else I prove !'

Low fell her head upon her breast
When thus her sin she had confest,
Nor seen one pausing there to rest—

A pilgrim father in his gown,
Dusty and travel-stained and worn ;
And as he heard the tears ran down,

'Daughter,' he said, 'thou art the snare
That Satan sets for a soul rare
Which nought could tempt that is less fair.

'If thou wouldst save it for Christ's fold,
Cut close thy hair of yellow gold
And change thy raiment new for old.

'Still more : thy love thou must conceal,
Indifference must feign to feel.
The task is hard, but for his weal

'Thy love thou canst forego, and bear
Pangs which at first he too will share,
But in the end the crown will wear

'Which saints and martyrs only gain
When torture fires and racks of pain
Have cleansed their souls from every stain.

'This crown can come through thee alone.
Bear thou thy cross and make no moan ;
So shalt thou all thy sins atone.'

She cut her hair of gleaming gold,
She clothed herself in sackcloth old,
She said, 'My pulses have grown cold ;

' I love but God alone.'   He heard,
Her lover fond, whose blood was stirred
Like quivering flame at every word.

' What lying priest hath wrought me this,
To rob me of the heavenly bliss
For which I gladly heaven would miss ?

' Not for thy locks of virgin gold,
Not for thy garment's purple fold,
Do I thy supple beauty hold

' Above all joys of earth or heaven ;
And though my sins were seven times seven
Thy love would prove the saving leaven ! '

Her eyes told what no words confest,
' If love will save thee thou art blest ; '
Firm as a saint she said the rest :

' Go ! follow duty day by day !
Since thou art saved if I obey
I will not lead thy soul astray.

' Then at our death we shall be shriven ;
Through Hades we shall pass to heaven ;
Since unto such as love too much
Much also is forgiven.'

CHAFF AND WHEAT.

'The blows that strike deepest into the heart are struck by human hands which we have loved and trusted.'

MY heart lay on the threshing-floor :
    I stifled every wail
As blow on blow descended
    From one who held the flail.

My heart lay on the threshing-floor,
    But it was not in vain ;
The chaff was scattered to the winds
    In hours of keenest pain.

My heart lay on the threshing-floor ;
    Yet, bruisèd though it be,
It still a worthy offering is
    To thee, beloved, to thee !

Then take it now and guard it well,
    Dear love, for love of me :
My heart lay on the threshing-floor
    That it might worthier be.

LOVE AND FAME.

'To be great is to be exposed to all the shafts of envy ; but to love is to wear an "armour against fate." '

I DREAMED.

Before me stood a vision bright,
A creature of celestial light,
Of glorious mien and mould.
Her velvet robe, with hem of gold,
Fell to her feet in graceful fold,
Gleaming with jewels rare and cold.
Her dark hair shaded lovely eyes,
Which flashed like stars in midnight skies
While, stately as a crownèd queen,
She wore her wreath of laurel green.
In reverence I bowed my head,
And saw, low kneeling by my bed,
A gentler, fairer, sylph-like form,
Whose eyes with love were beaming warm.
She spoke—her voice was sweetly low ;
In s lver tones it seemed to flow :

'Turn not away from heart like mine:
  With pulses warm and true ;
Turn not away that glance of thine
  Though bright yon form to view.
Her path is through a weary way ;
  Sharp thorns will pierce thy feet,
And falsely flatt'ring is the lay
  Thy list'ning ear will greet.
The canker eateth at her heart,
  It gnaweth to the core ;
Oh, bid her from thy side depart
  And never tempt thee more.
There's poison in the laurel leaf
  That's braided in her hair ;
Her very smile will bring thee grief
  Although it seems so fair.
Thy brightest hopes will all decay,
  Thy joys to ashes turn,
While in thy breast with fitful sway
  Their smouldering embers burn.'
The low voice ceased. I raised my eye
From hers, as blue as azure skies,
And turned them from her glance so warm
Upon the stately, radiant form.

The dark eyes smiled—entrancing gaze!
How fast my heart beat 'neath their rays!
The red lips moved—melodious flow!
Deep-toned as bugle notes drawn low,
They thrilled my heart with bounding
    throe.
  ' My name is Fame,' the goddess said ;
    ' My mission unto thee.
  A glory round thy path I'll shed
    If thou wilt go with me.
  The way is steep, a stony path ;
    But, when we gain the end,
  I'll crown with glittering coronal
    The brow that thou wilt bend.
  The world will turn an envious gaze
    Upon thy lofty height,
  And thou shalt proudly meet those rays
    And glory in thy might.
  Then come with me ; leave yonder fay
    To minds of meaner mould ;
  Come, on our path away, away,
    Success awaits the bold.'
That clarion voice awoke a lyre ;
It filled my veins with molten fire

As one by one its chords were swept.
I turned to Love ; she, kneeling, wept ;
Her lashes long drooped low with tears,
And 'neath their lids were boding fears.
'Look ere we part,' she sighing said ;
And then her hand my vision led;
I saw through fields of pulsing air
A pathway radiantly fair :
Green were the grots and mossy glades,
Cool flowed the rills in greener shades,
And wild flowers grew in tangled maze
Beneath the thick vine's arching ways.
The velvet turf was gemmed with dew,
And starry flowers of every hue,
And flute-like voices stirred the air
From loving lips of beings fair.
The path swept to a river's side,
Where timidly upon the tide,
With foot advanced, its power they tried ;
The amber wavelets gently bore
The spirit forms from verdant shore :
And oh ! entrancing, rapturous sight !
The banks beyond of crystal bright,

Wreathed with rich vines of emerald green,

And flowers so rare no eye hath seen,

And gates of sapphire and of gold,

And streets of pearl, and fountains cold,

While angel forms came forth to greet

The angel spirits which they meet.

' I'll go with thee, dear Love,' I cried ;

And still for glorious Fame I sighed.

Love marked the wildly-heaving sighs,

She saw the tears gleam in my eyes,

And, pointing with her faultless hand,

Said, ' Look at yonder toiling band.'

I looked ; and lo ! 'midst rocks and briers,

'Midst nameless graves and funeral pyres,

Fame's toil-worn band were struggling on

Beneath the fierce rays of the sun—

No mossy glades, no vine-arched ways,

To shelter them from burning rays ;

Their sunken eyes gleamed wild and strange,

And frequent looks of hate exchanged.

Upward and onward still they pressed,

While some, more weary than the rest,

Found by the way an unknown grave,

For not one stopped to soothe or save,

But, often trampling on the weak,
The highest place they seemed to seek.
They paused not for the dying wail,
The cheek so wan, so ashen pale ;
And, shuddering at the fearful sight,
I turned away in dread affright.
For Fame no more my spirit sighed ;
Ambition's power that moment died.
I follow Love, and Fame may flee—
No longer she hath charms for me.
Pale Envy's shafts at her are borne,
While Love escapes with armour worn
That clothes the form from crown to heel,
Invulnerable as proven steel.

THE SOUL'S CITADEL.

FROM AN UNPUBLISHED NOVEL.

I STOOD upon the heights of Love :
The air was passion-free ;
I thought not of the things of Time,
But of Eternity.

And he who led me to those heights,
And bade me scale its walls,
I looked upon as on a god,
As free from earthly thralls.

I scaled the walls, I reached the tower,
I flung my flag on high ;
I thought I heard the angels call
As breeze on breeze swept by.

My head was strong, my heart was brave,
My vision keen and clear ;
I saw the ways the saints have trod,
I felt their spirits near.

What foe would dare in hours like these
   A soul so clad assail?
Ah, woe is me! no foe but he
   Who helped me don my mail.

His hand struck low in cruel blow
   The one whose feet he'd led
From level plains to mountain-tops,
   And left me as one dead.

But still I hold my pure white flag,
   Though low in dust I lie;
I hear the breezes out of heaven
   Still murmur, murmur by.

And now 'tis given me to know,
   And see with spirit's eyes,
That Christ alone can lead our souls
   Up into Paradise.

THE STORY OF MY LOVE.

WHEN the lilacs were in bloom,
  And the skies were soft and pale,
I told my love the story
  As we walked in Thornleydale;
Oh, the aisles of lilac bloom
  In the green and lovely vale
Where I walked with Maud at morn,
  And she listened to my tale.

Twice six moons had waxed and waned,
  Twice six months had passed away,
Ere I begged my Maud to name
  Very near our wedding day.
So we walked in Thornleydale,
  While she, blushing, hung her head:
The moss roses on the bush
  Blush not half so sweet a red.

When the locusts were in bloom,
  Lilies pure and snowdrops pale
With my bride upon my arm
  I went out from Thornleydale;
Tender eyes were raised to mine,
  Tender lips to mine were pressed,
And I bore my bride away
  From her fair and flowery nest.

When the winter skies were grey,
  And the snow lay in the vale,
When the winds were bleak and wild,
  We came back to Thornleydale;
But the tender eyes were closed,
  And the tender lips were cold;
And my baby and my bride
  Sleep together side by side.

THE CUP OF LIFE.

I HOLD with trembling hand the full, rich cup
Which God has given unto me to drink—
Such generous dole that not one added drop
Could fall within and not o'erbrim its wealth.
I would my hold were stronger, but, alas!
The strongest arm is weak indeed against
The purposes of God. Ah! blest be he
Who still can give God thanks when all the wine
Life yields is spilled, and nought is left but lees.
Couldst thou, my heart? What didst thou do but
  moan
When on a time a north-east wind did breathe
Upon thy calm, vexing thy life with plaints
That would have best befit a tempest storm?
But now the wind has lulled, 'tis well and wise
To search thy soul and question of its strength,
That if again a few drops from thy cup
Are swept unto the ground, thou shalt not grieve

As if the richness of thy draught were gone.
Take time to thank thy God for what He leaves,
Faint heart, and thou wilt find the hours grow few
Wherein thou mournest over what He takes.

REAL AND IDEAL.

No storied castle's window owns a view
    Fairer than mine that overlooks the west ;
Rolling between are countless waves of blue,
    Bearing white sails unto their ports of rest.

Here slopes the orchard with its wealth of bloom,
    The cattle grazing to the water's edge ;
There stroll fair children on the shell-strewn beach,
    Or watch the scene from yon bold, beetling ledge.

Now curves the sinuous rock-bound coast away,
    Or reaches out in promontories fair,
While far beyond the tireless billows play
    And toss their white arms in the golden air.

Nearer, a meadow rolls its emerald sward,
    Flecked with white clover as with pearls of Ind,
Its huge breast scarred with timbers of the nord—
    Wrecks driven on shore in gales of adverse wind.

Where walls of rock relentless keep at bay
   The reckless waves that chafe against their sides,
Fall glowing showers of soft prismatic spray :
   As ceaseless break the never-resting tides.

I close my eyes : the meadow, coast, and wave,
   Like phantom pictures fade and disappear ;
Sweet absent faces gather round my own,
   And clinging hands clasp mine which are not
     here.

NEWPORT.

WORDS.

WHEN thought holds empire in the brain of man,
And deeds unworthy we are brought to scan,
How leaps the soul with indignation stung!
How words that burn find utterance on the tongue!
When Treachery strikes the heart with coward
    blow,
And Falsehood strives her subtle dart to throw,
The soul speaks up most nobly in its scorn,
Unless its clay be but ignobly born.
Not so when love falls wounded to the dust,
Smitten by hands it only knew to trust;
Words then are worthless to the anguished mind;
Save 'Help us, God,' no other words we find;
And but His strength upheld us in our need
We would be weak and powerless indeed.

DRIFTED AWAY.

IN the morn of life I anchored a barque
By some isles I was sure would stay ;
Alas ! alas ! in the treacherous dark
My green isles drifted away.

And now I look back on their groves of palm,
Their fountains of solace and joy,
As martyrs look for the life beyond
When flames and the rack destroy.

Bore ever a martyr a keener pain
Than our Lord when deserted knew ?
Can the fire scorch as burns the thought,
' I trusted to love not true ' ?

Come back, come back, my beautiful isles,
That I anchored my barque beside ;
No other isles like my isles of palms
In the tropic seas so wide !

Ah, when once an isle has drifted away,
  Nor fountains nor palms remain.
My anchor swings loose to lodge as it may ;
  My barque is at sea again.

RESIGNATION.

SHE heard the anguished wail of those whose hearts
Are broken on God's wheels, and when she said
To him who led her steps, ' Why bring me here ? '
He answered, ' Have no fear ; I do but lead
Where He directs who knows the path you need.'
Her trembling heart in terror tried to turn ;
But flaming swords, the ministers of fate,
For ever held her back, nor ceased pursuit
Until upon the rack, her heart, bound fast,
Writhing in torture lay.   Her ashen lips
Refused to say, ' Thy will, my God, be done ! '
And only murmured, ' Thine, O God, the power ! '
Then groaned the wheel, revolving round,
Till drop by drop the blood no longer flowed ;
For first like gushing fountains it poured forth,
Showering accusing spray in drops on those
Who lent their strength to turn its ponderous weight.
With life at lowest ebb God's angels came,
And one, whose face was radiant with peace,

Lifted her up and said, 'Come now with us,
Nor grudge the pain that wrung unwilling drops
From thy heart's core, since unto thee is given
To walk on earth with angels sent from heaven.'

THE ARMOUR OF LOVE.

'I.pity, I forgive, I forget.'—LOUIS XVIII.

YOU ask me whence the armour came
That steeled me through those days to live
He sent it who has taught me since
    To pity and forgive.

You ask me how I bore the cross
Ere recompensing crown was set ;
I like not to recall those hours :
    Would that I could forget !

You tell me now I know my friends ;
I knew them all, dear love, before ;
The phalanx never broke nor swayed
    . That Friendship's banner bore

You tell me that henceforth my life
Is freed from Envy's vengeful eye.
Believe it not ; till heaven is gained
    Her arrows still will fly.

E

But yet one word for you I have :
This armour that's around me wrought
Not only keeps her shafts from me,
    But makes them all as nought.

Draw as she may her monstrous bow,
With poisoned arrows basely set,
They cannot pierce the mail I wear,
    Since now I pity and forget.

PEACE THAT PASSETH UNDER-STANDING.

WHAT land of promise this that now I tread
What skies are these that, arching o'er my head,
Seem full of angel faces looking down,
As close I hold Love's sceptre and Love's crown ?
I have not crossed the barrier stream of death ;
Still does the mortal hold within its sheath
Its spirit body as the ripened husk its wheat ;
Still this sweet world I walk with clinging feet,
Loth to depart, yet longing still to go ;
Two natures warring each with each still flow
Like tides that now advance and now recede,
As earth attracts or heaven's voices lead.
The answer comes as if from God's white throne :
' Here dwell those hearts which my great peace
    have known.'

THE STRANGER.

'Abide with us ; for it is toward evening, and the day is far spent.'—LUKE xxiv. 29.

THE morning splendours of my life have flown,
   The noontide glories now are on the wane ;
I walk the path to Emmaus all alone,
   And think o'er 'things that happened' once
      again.

Who is the stranger joins me on the way,
   Teaching me truths which make my heart to
      . glow ?
O Lord, reveal Thy face to me, I pray ;
   If Thou art with me, give me sight to know

So the apostles walked with Him of old,
   And knew Him not until they sat at meat.
Methinks my loving heart would soon have told,
   Had I been there when He drew near to greet

I will not let a doubt within my soul
   That it is other than the Lord I love.
He leads me onward to yon distant goal ;
   I see the lights far streaming from above.

Abide with me ! my day is wellnigh spent ;
   The night of death, dear Lord, will soon be
      here ;
If on Thy breast whene'er the message's sent,
   What will I know of darkness or of fear ?

The morning splendours of my life have flown
   Its noontide glories now are on the wane ;
I walk the path to Emmaus *not* alone,
   For He is with me who of old was slain.

A PICTURE.

ONLY a churchyard covered with snow,
  A church in a lonely dale ;
There gleamed in the west a golden glow,
  The heavens above were pale.   .

The sentinel trees, like shades of the dead,
  Stood up stark against the sky :
Their frozen branches at rest were spread,
  For no winds went surging by.

The ground was white as the pure cold face
  That sleeps in its coffin-bed ;
A holy stillness was in the place
  That comes only to the dead.

To a longing wild my soul gave birth
  In that solemn peace to share,
To be done with the harsh turmoils of earth,
  Their pain and their wearying care.

'Would I were at rest!'   As the words arose,
  They died on my lips unsaid :
It seemed a sin before God to breathe
  I envied the buried dead.

I thought of him who stood by my side,
  The trials he had to bear,
Of the tender trust he had placed in me,
  Of the grief I had to share.

I wished no more for the frozen sleep
  Of the churchyard white and lone,
Where the ghostly trees their vigils keep,
  And winds in the midnight moan.

The picture hangs now in memory's hall—
  The churchyard covered with snow ;
And it holds my soul within its thrall
  In a spell that none can know.

'WOULD I WERE AT REST.'

'He chooseth best
Who chooseth labour instead of rest.'
H. B. BOSTWICK.

No readiness to die so pleaseth God
   As readiness to live to do God's will :
He measureth unto us appointed days;
   Our round of duties we have yet to fill.

Shrink not the task!   We can the victory win.
   Our fetters strong?   Our souls are stronger yet.
God did but fashion this pulsating clay
   In which the jewel of the soul to set.

That has dominion over flesh and sin.
   If the sore struggle be but once begun,
He'll give His angels charge concerning us
   Until the final victory be won.

Then let our lives a daily offering be;
   The incense sweet unto our God shall rise;
The contrite spirit and the humble heart
   He loveth better than the sacrifice.

LEAVING STOCKHOLM, MARCH 1874.

O WINGÈD winds! bear on the hours
   Which now for days must roll,
Dragging their weary length along
   Like nights within the pole—

The Arctic pole, where never sun
   Illumes for months the sea,
Though brightly shine the stars above,
   The stars of destiny.

In them I'll trust, for God is just,
   And orders all aright;
He holds the stars within their course
   From darkness unto light.

The winter goes, the summer comes,
   Then steadfast shines the sun;
For all the wintry nights are o'er
   And wintry days are done.

Now unto my desponding soul
    Its dearest hope I'll hold—
That steadfast love may centre round
    The darlings of my fold ;

That they may know no wintry days,
    No nights of dark despair ;
But o'er the tropic seas of love
    Float into havens fair.

When winter goes, may summer come,
    And steadfast shine the sun,
And all the wintry days be o'er,
    And wintry nights be done.

MIDWAY.

MIDWAY upon Life's sea my bark speeds on ;
Steeped with the noontide's gold, the cradled crests
I turn to look upon lie still as babes
Upon their mother's breast.   Ah! once it was
Not thus.   I know a time when wild storms raged,
And thick clouds swept athwart the sky, until
The waves, high tossed, in murky blackness fumed.
Some treasure from my hold I lost ere those
Rough waves grew calm ; some garnered hopes,
     some faith,
Some trust, went down, and for my loss my soul
Sent up a cry which might have pierced the
     heavens,
So sharp its agony.   But now the sea
Holds not one trace of all that wild turmoil.
I stand and gaze upon its vast expanse,
And strive to keep in view the far-off shore,
Which to my sight grows dimmer every hour—
The shore whereon I lingered ere my sails

Were trimmed, for pastime gathering pebble stones,
Which, Midas-touched, have turned since then to
   gold.
What of the land beyond ?   A dim grey haze
Rolls dense between, which, when the storms
      come on,
Lifts for a space, swift driven before the wind,
Revealing glimpses of a glorious haven.

*   *   *   *   *   *   *   *

I fear not tempests nor the blasts of cold
That sweep from frozen zones; these have no power;
But when I slowly drift through odorous groves
Of spice, soft languors wooing me to stay,
'Tis then I fear ; for if I leave my helm
For dalliance in those bowers, against some rock
It straight may graze, and leave a shattered bark,
Which, if I trust, will founder on the deep ;
Or if, at most, it bear me into port,
How would I dread to render my account
To Him who trusted to my hands the bark
He fashioned with such care, for purpose wise
And kind! O Father! grant through storm and calm
I still may near those shores where evermore
Thy angels stand to lead us up to Thee.

TO ONE WHO DISLIKES FLOWERS.

WHAT memories bring they unto thee,
That thou shouldst turn from flowers ?
What memories from beyond the sea,
From thy far northern bowers ?
Ah! well I know some mighty grief
Hath crushed from out thy soul
The love thou surely must have felt
Ere girlhood won its goal.
Say not that they were never dear :
I could not bear that sound ;
'Twould break the atmosphere of light
That now enfolds thee round.

I'd rather think some sacred grief,
Some buried love, may be,
Which, linked in memory with flowers,
Springs up in agony
Whene'er their gentle breath sweeps near,
Or when thy true eyes rest

Upon Earth's sweet and stainless buds,
  Her holiest gift, her best.
The 'jasmine' sweet, blue violets wild,
  I plucked with tender care,
Mingling their bloom with brighter hues,
  Exotics wondrous, rare.
I thought to see thee bend those eyes,
  So glorious in their light,
Most fondly o'er the treasured flowers ;
  But to my questioning sight
There came no pleasure to thy lips,
  No smile within thy eyes,
And coldly, coldly to my heart
  I held its great surprise.
The world may whisper thoughts unkind,
  But ne'er will I believe
Other than this : that thy strong heart
  In bitterness doth grieve
O'er some sad memory of the past,
  Some faded human flower,
For which of love thou still hast kept
  A more than regal dower.

DESERTED.

ALL night upon my bed I toss,
All day I sigh and moan ;
Ah ! wherefore should I break my heart
Against a heart of stone ?

She rolleth past me in the street
With all her pomp and show,
She leaneth on her cushioned seat
Unmindful of my woe.

Oh, cursed be he who came between
With his ill-gotten gold !
Oh, cursed—But no ; I dare not curse
The mother who hath sold

Her daughter's form without her heart.
My God ! that form so fair
Which I had thought to call my own,
And all my pleasures share !

But neither gold nor gems were mine ;
  Yet with her by my side
I would have won a prince's dower
  To deck my bonnie bride.

Alas ! alas ! what need have I
  To struggle with these hands ?
Without her smiles, oh what to me
  Are untold gold or lands ?

Oh, cursed—No, no; I will not curse:
  Peace rest with thee, my love;
Let me the only sufferer be,
  Poor caged and pinioned dove.

Though other arms your form enfold,
  I know within your breast
The memory of our hallowed days
  Must there for ever rest.

And though you school your eyes to scorn,
  And check the heaving sigh,
There cannot be but tears for me
  When others are not nigh.

F

A VALENTINE.

FAIR as the vestals, as serenely cold
   Art thou, sweet maiden, with thy eyes of blue ;
Thy tresses long, in waves of burnished gold,
   Cast shadows o'er a cheek of rose-leaf hue.

The silken lashes of thy violet eyes
   Drop with a sunny curve from snowy lid,
Half shading all the purity that lies
   Within their quiet depths so sweetly hid.

The matchless arching of thy ruby lip,
   The glittering pearls thy smile discloses,
Thy mouth fresh as the dew the flowers sip,
   And redolent of sweets as budding roses—

Too fair for my unskilful hand to trace,
   Never a poet could thy charms combine,
Nor artist draw thee in thy winning grace
   Unless a monarch of his art divine.

For such a boon how dare my heart aspire ?
　Trembling, I bring its wealth of love to thee ;
No Persian worshipper of flaming fire
　E'er bent his god a more devoted knee.

IN EGYPT.

My childhood's dream, the Orient reached,
  Why yearns my heart for home?
And why across the throbbing seas
  Do all my fancies roam?

Never before, except in dreams
  Or painter's glowing skill,
Such scenes have broken on my eyes
  Or made my pulses thrill.

Oh, witching hours! oh, days of light!
  Oh, nights of solemn calm
That float us down the storied Nile,
  Along its groves of palm!

Here Moses lived, and Joseph ruled,
  And Israel pitched his tent ;
Here came the Virgin with her Child,
  By angel voices sent.

Here art and science made their home,
　And skill and power reared
The monuments that mock at time,
　In grandeur vast and weird.

But though their majesty I feel,
　Still yearns my heart for home,
And still across the throbbing seas
　Will all my fancies roam.

THEBES, *February* 1866.

TO A STUDENT.

I HAD a dream for thee when thou wert young,
For e'er thy boyhood's years were scarcely told
I marked thy worth, and felt my pulses thrill
With thoughts of what thy future might reveal.
Press on, and make that vision of my mind
Complete. Press on, and scale those battlements
Wherefrom the conqueror looks forth on fields
Unstained with blood, elate with victory
Such as crowned emperors who spent their days
In carnage never knew. Elate, and yet
As humble as a child. No fruitless tears,
Like those that Alexander shed of old,
For other worlds to win ; for whoso takes
That wondrous citadel can from its walls
Count tier on tier of battlements to scale
Before his eager eyes will scan the broad
Arcana of great Nature's laws. And thus
The conqueror grows a child, and wears with grace
The garments of humility. 'Tis those,

And only those, who in dark trenches make
Faint passes with a play-time sword, nor reach
Beyond, who boast their prowess.   Take thou
    heed:
Sleep not upon thy post, so thou wouldst prove
Thyself a warrior worthy of the cause.
God give thee armour proof against assault
In whatsoever guise it come to thee,
Rounding thy life with every joy that makes
Complete the days of man, and grant that when
Thou layest down thy helmet and thy steel
'Twill be to take up worthier beyond.

MY HEART.

My heart is like a wild bird;
  'Tis ever on the wing,
Soaring amidst the amber clouds,
  A wild and wayward thing,
Or stooping to the green earth
  To nestle in some flower,
Or singing sadly all the day
  In some neglected bower.

My heart is like the wild wind ;
  It flitteth here and there—
Now wailing o'er some ruined shrine,
  Some cloister dim and bare,
Or laughing with the sunny sky,
  Or dancing with the rills,
Or sweeping through the brave old woods
  That crown the mossy hills.

My heart is like the wild stream
  That glideth through the vale,

Where grow the meek-eyed violets,
   The lilies pure and pale ;
Oh, this is what my heart is like,
   For, ever mirrored there,
Is some dear, stainless, cherished flower,
   Some bright bud sweet and fair.

And 'tis not like the wild bird,
   And 'tis not like the wind;
The bird is faithless to the flowers,
   Nor trust nor love can bind.
The wind full oft doth break their hearts,
   Surely they fade though slow ;
But the glad stream is always true
   To the flowers drooping low.

ANTICIPATION.

OH, hasten on, ye loitering hours!
I long once more to see
The valley of my childhood's home,
The mountains and the lea ;
The feathery groves that crown the hills,
Or droop beside the stream ;
The meadows green, the murmuring rills,
Where dewy violets gleam ;
The winding path around the lake
Where water lilies float,
And spread at eve their stainless sails
Like some sweet fairy boat ;
The dark grey rocks that on me frowned
From mountain ramparts bold,
The placid stream that glides below
Over its sands of gold ;
The village church with towering spire,
The elms upon ' the green ; '
The homesteads with their garden walks,
And verdant lawns between.

All, all, my fancy longs to see,
    Each spot within that vale ;
The graveyard with its mossy stones,
    And sculptured marbles pale.
All hold for me their memories
    Sacred as saintly shrines,
And like a pilgrim's longing heart
    My heart with longing pines.
But like a pilgrim at a tomb
    In silence I should bow,
If midst those scenes and in those haunts
    My feet should wander now.
Yet hasten on, ye loitering hours,
    That I may once more see
The valley of my childhood's home
    Ere earth is nought to me.
And when my busy brain is still,
    My heart has ceased to beat,
Then take me back, and bury me
    Where roamed my childish feet ;
And write upon a simple stone,
    That those who pass may read :
' *She was well loved* by God and man
    In hour of sorest need.'

BETRAYED.

SLOWLY stern Winter treads our hill-girt vale,
His regal brow with hoary locks encrowned ;
Through leafless trees he breathes a dirge-like
wail,
And the far hills repeat the mournful sound.

The bright-eyed flowers have paled beside the
stream
That winds across the fields its fitful way,
But from the woods I catch a crimson gleam
Deep as the glowing hues of dying day.

'Tis where the pliant vine entwines the oak,
Then upward climbs, wreathing from bough to
bough,
Falling beside the roof whose curling smoke
Alone I see above the forest now.

Thick gleam the sprays with coral berries fair,
    Its leaves as glossy as June laurels be ;
I knew a maid who ofttimes in her hair
    Braided its clusters all too carefully.

It is a story long and full of grief,
    That on this page I would not care to tell.
She faded with the summer flowers brief,
    When autumn's frosts first on their beauty fell.

Ah ! where is he who cast this deadly blight ?
    Hath he no share in sorrow he hath wrought ?
Can he escape the voice within by flight—
    The memories with such desolation fraught ?

Breathe to him, winter winds, of all the woe
    The mother feels within her lonely cot ;
Leave the new grave beside the river's flow,
    And whisper of the clay he hath forgot.

Oh, haunt him with thy wail, thou winter wind,
    And fill his sinful heart with boding fear ;
Give him no rest, let him no mercy find,
    Until he sheds the penitential tear.

Perchance it may some other victim save
    That even now his passion marks for prey ;
For little cares he, so that in the grave
    His sins are hidden from the light of day.

O Earth ! so fair art thou we scarce can dream
    Of all the sorrows hid within thy breast,
The broken hearts that cross dark Lethe's stream
    Ere thy fond bosom folds them to their rest.

Rest to the dust consigned unto thy care,
    While, far from thee, the spirit wings its way,
Fettered no more by chains it erst did wear
    Within its helpless tenement of clay.

Wail on, ye winter winds, above the dead ;
    Ye cannot wake her from her dreamless sleep ;
Soft is the pillow to her wearied head,
    For ever closed the eyes that once did weep.

A GIFT OF FLOWERS.

O FLOWERS of wondrous loveliness !
   What mem'ries strange arise
As all your beauty rich and rare
   I drink with eager eyes !

O meadows of my childhood's home !
   O forests dark and deep !
O mountains where I used to roam
   Far up the rock-crowned steep !

I see them all ; I feel the wind
   Playing amid my hair ;
I even scent the very breath
   Of violets on the air.

No others have seemed half so sweet
   Since from that spot I strayed ;
No others half so fair to me
   As those in that wild glade.

I hear the babbling torrent leap,
  I feel a hand in mine ;
Again I stray in those green paths
  As once in 'auld lang syne.'

But heavy, heavy grows the air,
  A mist creeps o'er my view ;
Dear saints ! I see my buried friend :
  Those are her eyes of blue !

Ah me ! ah me ! 'twas but a dream :
  The flowers alone remain ;
She knoweth all the bliss of heaven,
  And I of earth the pain.

The pain ! What said I, when my friends
  Strew o'er my path with flowers ?
Ah ! earth hath very much of joy
  To bless our passing hours.

And though these flowers fair will droop
  And wither soon away,
I shall keep always in my heart
  The fragrance of this day.

THE FAITHLESS LOVER.

'There, there will be neither marrying nor giving in marriage,
for we shall all be like the angels of God.'

SWEETEST Marion, wilt thou listen
   While my soul calls out for thine ?
Canst thou listen from high heaven
   To this longing prayer of mine ?
Oh, my love, am I no longer
   Friend of friends, dear one, to thee?
Can I have no word of answer ?
   Speak, pure soul, oh speak to me !

By our long and fond communings,
   By remorseful pangs I feel,
By the gnawings of this serpent
   In the wounds that will not heal,
By my love so strong and deathless,
   Though so faithless in that hour
When Ambition's torch still lured me,
   Held by hands that knew its power.

G

Bend thine earnest eyes upon me—
    Eyes so pure I can but weep
When I think that earth hath lost them,
    Well-like eyes so clear and deep.
Earth hath lost them, heaven hath gained them ;
    Oh, come back, thou angel form,
And my soul will go to meet thee
    From this world of grief and storm.

Ah ! I cannot feel thy presence :
    Death keeps guard between us now ;
He hath clasped thee since we parted,
    He hath kissed thy placid brow.
Death and falsehood came between us,
    But my spirit still is thine ;
And I know I am forgiven,
    Though I have no word nor sign.

When long years have passed before me,
    And my penance days are done,
I will seek through worlds eternal
    Till I find thee, cherished one.
There we'll need no vain betrothal,
    Like God's angels we shall be;
In thy eyes I'll read my pardon,
    Thou in mine my love for thee.

THE ENTHUSIAST.

O CRUEL heart that would my heart lay bare,
And seek with earthly love to spread a snare!
O spirit strong that would my spirit thrall,
And chain to earth its hopes and longings all!

I know thy power, yet hold myself to be
Able to triumph o'er the world and thee,
Renouncing earthly love if need require,
For in my heart there glows a holier fire.

Though troublous sorrows compass me around,
Though grief should leave its ever-bleeding wound,
Yet still my chosen path I'll persevere,
Nor hardships great nor hidden dangers fear.

Life hath ne'er been to me a field of flowers,
The world hath ne'er allured me to its bowers;
I find the thorn more quickly than the rose;
Seldom for me the buds their sweets disclose.

Sometimes they're touched by the untimely frost,
Sometimes by blight or hidden worm they're lost;
But though I mourn, my sorrow I restrain :
God loveth those to whom He giveth pain.

Renounce the world, its pomp, its gilded show,
And seek the well-springs of thy life to know ;
Its turbid waters will become more pure
When Sin and Folly's whirl no longer lure.

Renounce the world !   It yields nor peace nor .joy,
Nor aught of happiness without alloy;
Strive for the crown the humblest Christian wins,
And pray forgiveness for thy many sins.

For thee my heart will frequent plead in prayer;
Though strong its love, it shall not prove a snare :
I know thy power, yet hold myself to be
Able to triumph o'er the world and thee.

SONG OF THE FORSAKEN.

WHEN the flowers were in bloom
Justly proud our homestead stood,
Buried in the shadows cool
Of the silver maple wood ;

And the locust's lovely. plumes,
And the woodbines o'er the door,
And a wealth of leaf and bloom
Threw their shadows on the floor.

When the flowers were in bloom—
Never flowers half so fair
As those blossoms of my youth,
Raining fragrance on the air—

Never sward so emerald green
As the lawn that spread around—
Never roses half so fair
Shed their petals on the ground.

Ah, the roses! where are they?
Doth the summer bring them still,
Though the roses of my life
Never more shall bloom at will?

Is the woodbine's breath as sweet
Now as in the days of old?
Bloom the violets in the turf
And the crocus buds of gold?

Roses come and roses go,
Summer's warmth and winter's snow;
But no blossoms for her life
Who is neither maid nor wife!

THE APPROACH.

'It is sweet, gentle Death.'
        SINTRAM AND HIS COMPANIONS.

As I watch the moments go
My life runneth very low,
    Very near seems Death.
If he reachèd out his hand
From the place where he doth stand,
    He could stop my breath.

This is not the spectral form
Come to chill my pulses warm,
    And to seal my sight;
This is not the phantom grim
That I fancied Death had been:
    'Tis a form of light.

Tales they told me long ago;
Now I see they are not so,
    For his mien so fair:
In his arms I have not lain,
But I know that woe and pain
    Cannot reach me there.

ANSWER

TO THE HYMN

' Why thus longing, thus forever sighing
For the far-off, unattained, and dim,
While the beautiful all round thee lying
Offers up its low perpetual hymn ?'

Know you not that He who planted
  In our hearts this longing dim
Knew the unattained would draw us
  Ever nearer unto Him ?

Though the bee, and bud, and blossom
  Bring us lessons every day,
All in vain their gentle teaching
  If our work we turn away.

They whose lives are ever fruitful
  Are the ones who strive to know,
First, the duties lying near them,
  Next, to live for friend and foe.

Who so poor that hath not round them
   Thrown some rays of joy and light?
Who so lorn, so sad and weary,
   As to always dwell in night?

When the longing falls upon us
   Nothing can its chafings still :
He who made our hearts for loving
   Knows that nought but love can fill.

If the dear eyes are not near us
   For whose glance we thirst alone—
If we may not hear the voices
   That once answered to our own—

Is it sin to weep in silence
   (Wearing to the world a mask)
E'en while working for the Master
   Who apportions every task?

Though the fickle crowd applaud us,
   Though we find unsought renown,
We must bear our earthly crosses
   Till we win our heavenly crown.

If the fickle crowd breathes hatred,
  If it tears our laurels down,
'Tis not given to the worthless
  To take up the martyr's crown.

They who live to work for others
  Have not learned to live in vain ;
They who share the griefs of others
  Learn to lighten their own pain ;

And in listening to the teachings
  Of fair Nature's chanted hymn
Thus the restless yearning draws them
  Ever nearer unto Him.

LETTERS.

IN dewy shades the violet grows,
  Shedding its perfume sweet;
The passer-by with careless step
  Treads it beneath his feet.
But still its incense to the air
  With lavish waste is spread;
Bruised though it be, its sweetness rests
  Until the flower is dead.

But if some thoughtless hand should pluck
  The flower from its stem,
And hold it to the sun's hot rays,
  Where is its sweetness then?
So with the words of love that flow
  In written converse sweet—
If taken from their sacred shade
  The eyes of all to greet;
For ever flown their magic spell,
  No art can e'er recall
The heart's perfume that in them lies
  Which was not shed for all.

IT MIGHT HAVE BEEN.

RIGI wrapped in purple shadows,
  Pilatus bathed in dusky gold,
All the placid lake between them,
  And the peaks of mountains bold,
In the amber light of sunset
  Like a dream of heaven lay ;
But my heart was steeped in sadness,
  For its heaven was far away.

No more in the living present,
  But within the buried past,
Will my thoughts for ever wander,
  Like the ghosts in Hades cast—
Restless spirits that are tortured
  By the joys they cannot win,
Or the anguish that is written
  In these words : ' *It might have been.*'

LUCERNE.

GRIEF, CONSCIENCE, AND FAITH.

WITH Grief I stood one day so face to face
That every lineament my eyes could trace ;
Her cheeks were whiter than the drifting snow
Whereon no sunbeam throws a radiant glow,
She laid her marble hand upon my breast.
Good heart ! as fades the sunshine in the west,
Thereat the colours of my life grew pale,
And every joy and pleasure straight did fail.
'Ah, Grief !' I cried, 'what doest thou with me ?
For Christ's dear sake, O Grief! I pray thee, flee.'
' Ah ! but for Christ's dear sake I came,' she cried,
' To lead thee, wanderer, to thy Saviour's side.'
And so my bruised and bleeding heart we bore,
And laid the offering at the Saviour's door.

Then Conscience said, ' Is this a gift for Christ ?
The heart which friends have careless thrown
     aside,
Wounded and pierced, with earthly passions dyed,
All bruised and torn—is this a gift for Christ ? '

And trembling, I shrank back in mortal fear,
And answered, ' Nay, oh nay ; yet leave it here ;
For Christ Himself was once by friends betrayed,
And I will adjuration make,' I said.
' For pity's sake, though great indeed my sin
In loving creature more than loving Him,—
For pity's sake, He yet may hear my cry,
And stoop to lift me when He passeth by.'
Then Faith cried out, ' Oh ye of little trust,
Christ loves you most when humbled in the dust.'

THE COUNTRY.

My heart is light within me
  When the days are bright and long,
And my soul breathes forth its music
  As the bird trills forth its song.

My heart is light within me,
  For I love the woodland air,
And in these peaceful pine groves
  I have no thought of care.

All nature lies around me,
  Serene and calm and still ;
The blue sky bends above me
  To meet the arching hill.

And all amidst the space so wide,
  No human form I see
To break the holy solitude
  Of valley, hill, and lea.

And yet I never feel alone,
  Nor weary of the scene :
For far more dear than city spires
  Are these grand trees of green.

Bright orioles flash from bough to bough ;
  Their joyous notes they pour,
Sweet strains of gushing melody
  That drown the waters' roar.

For down in yonder dark ravine
  There falls a silvery stream ;
Tossing around the mossy rocks,
  Wild as a poet's dream.

Fair field flowers lift their fragile heads
  Where'er the eye doth fall ;
Amid the waving wheat and rye
  I see the poppies tall ;

Like coals of fire in embers pale
  Their brilliant blossoms glow ;
And drifting all along the lanes
  The daisies spread their snow.

Ah! not with birds and brooks and flowers
Could I e'er feel alone ;
For always in wild Nature's haunts
My sweetest joys are known.

And to our God, who made this earth
So beautiful and fair,
My heart sends up its offering
Of ceaseless praise and prayer.

HOME.

OH peaceful home! how sweet within thy walls
　To watch the dying of the golden day,
Knowing that soon unto thy cheerful halls
　A loved one's smile will shed a brighter ray!
How fondly do I watch the changeful skies,
　Fading from crimson to the violet's hue,
And long for eve, that I may meet his eyes,
　Which, like the stars, shine steadily and true!
Oh happy home! how much with pleasure fraught
　Are all the changing scenes thou bring'st to me!
How much of joy that I had never thought
　Could in this world of disappointment be!
Most gladly do I bring unto thy shrine
　The wild desires, the gilded hopes, of youth;
No more for dreamy visions shall I pine,
　Sure of thy boundless and thy changeless truth.

Oh blissful home! what wonder that I sigh
　Lest some rude blow destroy these scenes so fair,
And Love, affrighted, spread her wings and fly,
　And leave me brooding o'er my own despair?

With trembling hand I seek to draw the veil
  Which hides the future from my earnest gaze ;
But, like a far and fast receding sail,
  Pale shadows glide into the distant maze.
Oh earthly home! my spirit feels how frail.
  Are all the ties which bind it here to thee—
How much of sorrow in this tearful vale!
  How much of storm upon life's treacherous sea!
And if the bark which we have launched with care
  Before these angry storms be wildly driven,
Oh grant, my God, the fragile wreck may bear
  Its precious freight to the blest *home of Heaven.*

GRAND-CHILDREN.

I HASTEN to my hallowed room
  When twilight shadows fall,
Where faces that I love the best
  Look on me from the wall.

But not for their dear smiles alone,
  In silent welcome sweet ;
It is to listen to the sound
  Of pattering little feet.

They gladden but a neighbour's home,
  Yet through the kindly wall
The happy sound comes unto me,
  I hear each soft footfall.

And here I sit and close my eyes,
  And think how, o'er the sea,
Some little feet are pattering now,
  So very dear to me.

Oh, far across the stormy sea,
　And far beyond the main—
So far my heart doth often ask,
　Shall we e'er meet again ?

And then the tears fall thick and fast ;
　My heart is like to break ;
I long to reach the little ones
　In my fond arms to take.

Oh, precious pets beyond the wall,
　Within the home you bless
No one looks on a vacant seat,
　None miss a lost caress.

But ever, as the days go by
　And twilight shadows fall,
The patter of your little feet
　Such memories recall,

That often I look wistfully
　To the Immortal shore,
Where tears and sorrows never come,
　And partings are no more.

MAUD.

To what shall I liken matchless Maud?
The queen of flowers that poets laud
      Cannot with her compare ;
No lily drooping in valley low
Where only purest of lilies grow
      Was ever half so fair.

Eyes that would shame the stars of night,
So pure their flashing depth of light,
      Yet shy as wild gazelle's ;
Lips of as rich and bright a dye
As carmine fields in Orient sky
      When chime the vesper bells ;

Cheeks of as rare a curve and mould
As ever shaped by sculptor old
      In palmiest days, I ween ;
And waves of silken, sunny hair
Shading the brow divinely fair
      Of our sweet household queen —

All these are hers ; and, ah ! we fear
Such charms, increasing every year,
    A dangerous dower will be.
God shield our little Maud from ill
Shall be our prayer, as ever, till
    We've crossed life's changeful sea.

THE MESSAGE.

' I have a presentiment of approaching evil.'

LETTER.

'TWAS yester eve I felt the same ;
  It is no longer so,
For rays of hope illume my heart,
  And shed within their glow.
Then scatter to the wind your fears,
  And bid your heart be strong ;
You hold your fate within your hands :
  Make not the right seem wrong.

Thy message, Heaven-sent to-day
  In answer to my prayer,
Has reassured my boding soul,
  And lifted all its care.
Henceforth I'll wait with patient trust :
  ' *Whatever is, is right ;* '
I will not murmur at His will
  Though clouds shut out the light.

And may He fill your life with joy,
    And round with love your days ;
Then, though our paths be far apart,
    Still will I render praise.
Now give unto the winds your fears,
    And bid your heart be strong ;
You hold your fate within your hands :
    Make not the right seem wrong.

COMPENSATION.

'Thou shalt be hidden from the scourge of the tongue.'

JOB V. 21.

FORGET not, Lord, Thy promises
　To those who trust in Thee ;
Close not Thy ears unto their cries,
　Nor from their presence flee.

For Thou art mighty in Thy strength,
　And we are weak and frail ;
To combat evil without Thee
　What would our powers avail ?

O Lord, how long must we endure,
　How long the scourge abide,
Before Thy arms shall fold us round,
　Thy love our sorrows hide ?

We plead the promises of old,
　Weary and faint we cry ;
Withhold not, Lord, thy sheltering grace
　When unto Thee we fly.

'Mortal! hope not while here on earth
　God's chastening rod to flee ;
Rather lift up thy heart in praise
　That *thus* He chasteneth thee.

'Not with fierce trials born of shame,
　Nor sorrows steeped in sin,
Hast thou to walk thy pilgrimage,
　His courts to enter in.

'He giveth thee thy every wish,
　Reserving *only one*—
To draw thee always near to Him,
　And to His Saviour Son.'

The still, small Voice was heard no more,
　But round me and above
God's holy angels seemed to float,
　And all was peace and love.

SYMPATHY.

'For a loving heart to lack sympathy is worse than pain.'
REV. F. W. ROBERTSON.

WHY should we fly to human aid
To tell our tales of woe,
When God's just ear is ever lent
Unto our cries below?

What solace can it give like His?
What strength whereon to rest
Like that we find at His dear feet *in hours of prayer*
When by our griefs opprest?

Teach me, my God, to turn to Thee
Whenever storms shall lower,
Remembering how weak is man,
How strong Thy gracious power.
My every grief *to Thee I'll bring,* at Thy dear feet,
My every care, I'll leave;
Thy love shall heal each bleeding wound;—
I shall no longer grieve.

HOW LONG?

How long, O Lord, how long?
  My weary soul makes plaint;
How long, Lord, wilt Thou hold
  Thy arms from those who faint?

My cause is Thine, O God!
  For justice, truth, and right
I looked to Thee for help,
  And trusted in Thy might.

I know that not in vain
  I place my hope in Thee,
That when Thy time is ripe
  Sure is my victory.

How long, O Lord, how long?
  My weary soul makes plaint;
Eternal truth and justice reign:
  Let not my heart grow faint.

A MEMORY OF THE NILE.

A steamer with the American flag passed our dahabeah, January 31, 1866, the passengers singing, 'Rally round the flag, boys.'

A DAY of calm : our sails were down ;
   The boatmen idly rowed ;
An azure sky without a cloud :
   The Nile scarce rippling flowed.

The palm groves stood against the sky,
   And not a leaf was stirred ;
The camels grazed amidst the fields,
   The shepherd watched his herd.

Women, with flashing Orient eyes,
   And garments flowing free,
Paused with their water jars erect
   The Frank's pale face to see.

Their turbaned lords reclined at ease
  In groups along the shore ;
Each scene a picture to our eyes,
  The day thus onward wore.

When, lo ! a steamer speeding past
  With Stars and Stripes on high !
Our hearts beat fast, our pulses thrill,
  Tears start from every eye.

The dear old flag ! So far from home,
  What memories it brings !
Straightway across the distant seas
  Our fancies spread their wings.

We seem to hear the bugle strains
  Of pealing battle hymns,
Which nerved our hearts to earnest work
  And kindled statesmen's themes.

We seem to hear—Oh no, for now,
  Swelling upon the air,
The very strains that fancy brought
  The morning wind doth bear.

O God! if thus the heart can leap,
  If thus the soul can thrill,
While denizens of earth we roam
  Where pleasure leads at will,

What must the life celestial bring
  When, on that heav'nly shore,
We see the dearest loved on earth
  Whom Thou didst call before,

And hear their voices on the air,
  Blent with the seraphs' song,
In strains of welcome unto those
  Who join their holy throng?

Eye hath not seen nor ear hath heard
  The joys that crown the blest,
For never unto mortal heart
  The least hath been confest.

But if, when in a foreign land
  Our wandering footsteps roam,
Our bodies scarce our souls contain
  When rings some lay of home,

Shall we not guess the finer joy
    Unto the spirit born
When from the night of death it soars
    To reach the heavenly morn ?

GENESEE FALLS.

On thy wild banks, O lovely Genesee!
  I stand entranced, gazing with calm delight
  Upon thy leaping waters, foaming white
Like wings of angels in their purity.
From the abyss curls upward the thin spray,
  As incense from some massive temple shrine,
  Bathing in ten-fold beauty shrub and vine,
And lingering there as though they wooed its stay.
Below, the stream glides onward tranquilly,
  Mirroring upon its fair and placid sheen
  The crested cliffs, with all their wealth of green,
Until it meets Ontario's inland sea:
There, there it falls most peacefully to rest
Like some worn child upon its mother's breast!

NIAGARA BELOW THE CATARACT.

WITHIN a temple's towering walls I stand—
A temple vast ; the heaven is its dome :
No corniced crag was hewn by human hand,
Nor by it wrought this tracery of foam ;
The inlaid floor of emerald and pearl
Heaves at the hidden organ's thunderous peal,
While round and up the clouds of incense curl,
Shrouding the chancel where the billows kneel.
Ah ! bow your heads. It is a fitting place
For solemn thought, for true and earnest prayer;
For here the finger of our God I trace,
Beneath, above, around me, everywhere.
He hollowed out this grand and mighty nave,
And robed His altar with the ocean wave

THE BROKEN TRYST.

I am weary, weary watching,
  For my watch is kept in vain ;
Broken is the tryst he made me ;
  Will he never come again ?

Floating clouds with sails of purple
  Glide along the eastern sky,
Freighted with the golden arrows
  That the sunset throws on high.

O'er the lake, by yon blue mountain,
  Sinks the Persian's god from sight,
And the western sky is flaming
  With his radiant paths of light.

Pathways paved with rubies glowing,
  Massive gates of gleaming gold,
Walls of jacinth, from which banners
  Float in soft and gorgeous fold.

* * * * * *

Now the stars in gentle glory
   Beautify the azure fields,
And the moon, in clouded chariot,
   Virgin queen, her tribute yields.

Wherefore does my loved one linger?
   Answer, peerless stars of light!
Tell me if his heart be constant,
   Though he keep no tryst to-night.

Ah! in vain, in vain I question;
   Hidden things may not be told;
Mortal lips may not hold converse
   With the silent stars of old.

I am weary, weary watching,
   For I watch, alas! in vain;
Broken is the tryst he made me,
   Broken is my heart with pain.

THE DYING WIFE.

'For death itself I did not fear ;
'Tis love that makes the pain.'—E. B. B.

OPEN the casement wide and give me air,
  And let me look once more upon the sky,
Once more upon my earthly home so fair,
  Once more before I die.

How gently doth the south wind fan my brow,
  Kissing the tresses damp with death's cold dew
How sweet the clustering flowers on yon green
    bough !
  The far-off heaven how blue !

More beautiful to me the earth doth seem,
  Now that I know the parting hour is near,
More terrible the sleep without one dream,
  The grave more dark and drear.

Clasp close the hand that hath not strength to
    press ;
Kiss, kiss the lips that soon will be so cold ;
Say when I'm gone you will not love me less
    Than in the days of old.

Beloved, it is a bitter thing to die,
    To feel the pulse grow weak while love is strong,
To know that dim and dimmer grows the eye
    That watched thy smile so long.

Ah ! earth hath been to me too much like heaven,
    Thy love hath made me prize my life too well ;
But earthly treasures are but lent, not given,
    As thy fond tears will tell.

Then let me die. I would not live to see
    Thy smile wax less, faint and more faint thy
        tone ;
Life would be worse than death, dear love, to me,
    If thou, my life, wert gone.

       *   *   *   *   *   *   *

Ah, there is neither death nor sorrow there,
    And God is love ; and love to us is given
To make our earthly life more passing fair,
    And more of bliss our heaven.

Farewell, farewell! I know my end is near ;

   Bend down beside me till I feel thy breath ;

God bless thee, love, when I'm no longer here :

   Oh, this indeed is death !

INVOCATION

SPIRIT of song, why droopest thou,
  Why foldest thou thy wing ?
Oh, stir anew within my soul,
  And strive to soar and sing.

Forget the ruined shrines of earth,
  The darksome cypress gloom,
'And stretch thy deep and searching gaze
  Beyond the dreary tomb.

Thus shalt thou gather strength to rise
  Above this troubled life,
Heedless of all its vain turmoil
  And all its wearying strife.

Thy steadfast eyes once fixed above,
  Serene as sunset glow,
And joyous as the forest birds
  Thy songs would ever flow.

No more thy grieving, mournful plaint
  Would echo in my breast,
But tones of joy would ever chant
  My troubled thoughts to rest.

Angels stoop low to bear thee up ;
  Resigned unto their sway,
Their wings shall cleave the arching blue
  As cleaves the mid-sun's ray.

Before the throne where seraphs bow,
  Beside the waters still,
And through the pastures fresh and green,
  Thou'lt walk with them at will.

Ah ! blest be God that hope and love
  And faith to us are given,
Angels to lift our souls from earth
  And ope the gates of heaven.

IN MEMORIAM.

THE MIDNIGHT VIGIL.

THE winds are holding carnival to-night,
  Driving their chariot clouds across the sky ;
Weird sounds are borne upon the troubled air
  As troop by troop ~~the pale~~ hosts hurry by.

They waken superstitions of my youth
  Which years ago I thought were lulled to rest,
When Reason took them in her matron arms
  And rocked them sleeping on her matron breast.

But now these sobs, once more upon the night,
  Fall as before in days so long ago ;
I seem to hear low voices murmur by
  In waves of sound as tides that ebb and flow ;

Are the pale spirits of the dead now loose,
  Calling for others their pale ranks to swell ?
Oh, pass us by within this loving home—
  Come not anear us with such purpose fell !

I keep my vigils by a sleeping form ;
  The tears fall ever from my watching eyes.
O God, in mercy grant he may be spared !
  Who could replace him in his counsels wise ?

Who could replace him in his tender love ?
  Who the great void could ever, ever fill ?
Ah, cease thy questionings, fond and feeble heart,
  And learn to wait upon God's holy will.

The wind in peaceful murmurs dies away ;
  A sacramental silence fills the air ;
The spirits of the just are round about,
  And God, in whom I trust, is everywhere.

December 1859.

AFTER THE VIGIL.

THEY told me time would deaden grief;
  And so I sat with folded hands,
And waited for the slow relief,
  And watched the hour-glass' glittering sands.

The days went by I knew not how;
  I only knew he was not here;
Morning and night were all the same,
  Morning and night alike were drear.

One thought I mused on o'er and o'er:
  'If love survives the grave,' I said,
'He will come back to us again;
  They cannot keep him with the dead.

'His every thought was for our weal;
  Can he so soon forget us there
As any happiness to know
  While our sharp cries still cleave the air?'

Then came thick clouds across my brain ;
　My faith and trust were lost in gloom ;
' This is the end of man ! ' I cried ;
　' All that once loved lies in the tomb ! '

Appalling thought !　My reason reeled ;
　Life seemed to me a cruel jest ;
I mourned the hour that gave me birth,
　And called upon the grave for rest.

God answered not my erring prayer,
　But gently took me by the hand,
And led me to the house of want,
　And whispered there His wise command :—

Go feed the hungry, bind the bruised,
　Speak to the dying words of cheer ;
So shalt thou feel within thy heart
　Thy heaven begun, though wandering here.

' So shalt thou feel his spirit still
　Ever in ministry with thine ;
Mortal, he is not lost to thee :
　He waits beyond the bounds of time.'

DEATH.

O WONDROUS sphinx ! within thy marble breast
  What undreamed secrets lie concealed !
Hast thou no pity for my wild unrest—
  My maddening longing for the unrevealed ?

As soon might I expect the stones to melt
  Beneath the vernal April's frequent rain ;
As soon might I expect thou wouldst relent,
  And give unto my arms my dead again.

' Blind on the rocks,' I stand, and stretch my hands ;
  Wearied and faint, unto my God I cry ;
Oh ! show to me these mysteries of Death,
  Even if them I too must die.

The days pass on.   He does not heed my prayer ;
  He still has work on earth for me begun ;
Ah, wondrous sphinx ! my lips will one day wear
  Thy smile of peace when all my work is done.

K

Then shall my soul escape these bonds of clay,
   Soaring through space to solve thy secrets old ;
Then shall my dead be given back to me ;
   Then shall the wisdom of my God unfold.

ISABEL.

'And Jesus called a little child to Him.'—MATT. xviii. 2.

WHERE have they led our little Bell,
　The firstling of the fold,
Who was rocked to rest
On her mother's breast
　So tenderly of old?

Where have they led our little Bell?
　Have they left her with the dead?
We miss the pure grace
Of her fair young face;
　Where was the sweet child led?

Down in the churchyard drear and lone,
　Was Isabel left there?
With marble cold cheek,
And hands folded meek,
　Like those of a saint at prayer?

No, not the graveyard drear and lone
  Holdeth our little Bell.
God opened His gate,
And the royal state
  Of her glory who shall tell?

The angels called her all the day,
  Our dear Lord led her in.
Why should we so weep,
When through gates of sleep
  A sweet child passeth from sin?

1856.

MEMORIES.

AGAIN I stand beside thy grave, my friend,
  Striving in vain to check these flowing tears;
Again above this emerald mound I bend,
  Recalling all our love in childhood's years.

Thy blue eyes, radiant with the spirit's light,
  Again beam on me as in days of yore,
Thy chestnut hair, thy brow so marble white,
  The tender smiles thy sweet lips ever wore.

Again I walk thy lovely form beside ;
  Hand clasped in hand, we rove from dale to dale,
And in the shade where flows the crystal tide
  We wreathe the ivy and the lilies pale.

'Tis but a dream; the cypress tree doth wave
  Its gloomy branches o'er thy cherished form,
And moaning night winds whisper round thy grave
  When through these dark pines sweeps the weep-
    ing storm.

Still grow the lilies in yon meadow green,

Still flows the streamlet o'er the silver sand ;

There's nought to miss from this fair woodland
scene,

But the soft pressure of thy clasping hand.

And thou, our fairest lily of the vale,

Hast faded, wilted, ceased, alas ! to bloom ;

Summer's soft breath can never aught avail

To raise our flow'ret from the turf-spanned tomb.

But, O my God ! I thank Thee for the faith

Which to my heart in mercy hath been given ;

For while I mourn a voice within me saith,

' Thy lily blooms more beautiful in heaven.'

A DIRGE.

STAINLESS lilies of the vale,
Fragile lilies, pure and pale,
   Slowly toll your snowy bells!
Hear ye not a mournful tale
In the zephyr's dying wail
   As it murmurs through the dells?

Meadow violets, meek and low,
White as any flake of snow,
   Closer bow your heads to earth!
Do you feel no pang, no throe,
~~Is there~~ See no sign by which you know
   A mortal's heavenly birth?

Song-birds by that forest side
Where the rippling waters glide,
   Breathe a slower, sadder strain!
For our hearts send up a plaint
Through our voices low and faint,
   And she answers not again.

Summer roses gemmed with dew,
Clouds that float o'er heaven's blue,
   All things pure and frail and fair,
Bring some offering to the grave
Where the dark pines nightly wave,
   For our loveliest sleepeth there.

AN ANNIVERSARY.

'The loveliest spot on earth.'

In hallowed silence let me keep this day
    Sacred to one whose home was erstwhile here,
Who hath escaped her pinioned bonds of clay,
    And with the angels roves from sphere to sphere.
We know that sorrow cannot reach her there ;
    We do not wish her back where tears are shed.
Within those regions gloriously fair
    Mysterious joys attend our sainted dead ;
The deepest bliss that earth can e'er bestow
    Hides wearing griefs too oft beneath it all ;
But in those realms no touch of care nor woe
    Upon the pure and ransomed spirit falls.

*   *   *   *   *   *   *

Only one year ago her home was here,
    And every bud and flower bloomed for her.
She watched the sails that glided far and near,
    The crested tide wooing the rocky shore,

The angel clouds that beckoned her away,
And all but one short year ago to-day.
How patiently she bore the rod of pain,
Yet plead for life because it was so dear!
Oh, suffering one, who now within the veil
Dost see thy Father's wisdom vast and clear,
Could we but know the glories of thy state,
How should we long to share them there with
thee!
How would our restless souls scarce deign to wait
The longed-for hour when Death shall set us free!
Canst thou not bend thy pitying eyes from heaven,
Filled with their mother-smile of tenderest love,
As shine the distant, holy stars of even,
From the deep richness of the realms above?

No; ask it not.   He knoweth what is best
Whose joys no eye hath seen nor tongue confest.

NEWPORT, *July* 13, 1868.

A TRIBUTE.

St. John's Church, Wilmington, Delaware,

Founded by Alexis I. du Pont.

NEVER of dust beneath did sculptured tomb
So eloquently speak as this grey spire
Of thee, O labourer without hire, whose day
Closed with the noon, thy Master calling thee
Straight from the field, before thy work was done,
To rest with Him above.   Before thy work
Was done?   We dare not say of thee, whose life
Was filled to overflowing with good deeds—
Who crowded labours in the noon-tide hour
So great as this—that aught was left undone.
No.   Blessed be He who set thee to thy task,
And when the hours of servitude were o'er
Redeemed the promise of our Christ, and called
Thee home to glories of thy heritage.

   *   *   *   *   *   *   *

These massive walls defy the hand of Time;

Long years shall pass and find them still secure ;
Green creeping vines will clamber o'er thy sides
And interlace their sprays.   The passers-by
Will feel with quickening hearts thy untold worth ;
And so to children's children will thy name
Go down, kindling to deeds of love men still
Unborn and scattering seeds for harvest-time.

AN AUTUMN SUNSET.

THESE amber clouds of autumn skies,
    Like islands of the blest,
Float on to my enraptured eyes
    Across the radiant west.
With crimson tints the saffron blends,
    Dark purple streaks the sky,
And snow-white masses floating up
    Like sails go gliding by.
The sun has vanished from my sight
    The twilight gathers round;
She casts the banners of the night
    Athwart the vestured ground:
And all the earth is calm and still;
    No sound falls on the ear
Save the low murmur of the stream
    That winds along the mere;
And down, far down, the deep ravine
    Some insect's plaintive cry,

And now and then a wild bird's call
  As flocks go swooping by.
Ah! in the silence of this hour
  How fast the memories throng!
While the tears will rise unbidden
  Although the heart be strong—
Tears which but one short twelvemonth since
  We little thought to shed,
For loving eyes smiled on us then
  That now are with the dead.
We miss the pressure of her hand,
  Her fond and gentle tone,
And wheresoe'er we turn our eyes
  We miss the love-light flown.
Oh, never can this earth put on
  The brightness erst it wore,
Nor autumn winds nor autumn skies
  The glories once they bore.

1851.

A PSALM OF THANKSGIVING.

How can I thank Thee as I would,
 O God! my God of grace!
Who from behind the gloom of death
 Reveal'st Thy smiling face?

How can I thank Thee as I would,
 O God! my God of love!
That Thou hast drawn those weary feet
 To rest in realms above?

How can I thank Thee as I would,
 O God! my God of peace!
That Thou didst send Thy messenger
 With painless, swift release?

I cannot thank Thee as I would,
 But make my life to be
A ceaseless offering of praise
 For ever, Lord, to Thee!

April 3, 1876.

'BABY ERNALD.'

O ACHING hearts, hold fast your pain!
O eyes that weep, your tears restrain!
The spirit flown comes not again.

Close the fringed lids to dreamless rest;
Fold the sweet hands upon the breast:
God ever knoweth what is best.

Not for our lost these tears that flow:
For us the bitter, bitter woe;
For him the bliss that angels know.

For us, we bear the anguished pain;
While for *our lost* we look in vain,
Through blinding tears that fall like rain.

———

Father! we know Thy pitying care!
Help us our aching hearts to bear!   .

1876.

'NOT LOST, BUT GONE BEFORE.'

'Ah, Christ, that it were possible
For one short hour to see
The souls we loved, that they might tell us
What and where they be.'

TENNYSON.

'O MY lost one! precious lost one!
How my heart cries out for thee,
Across the sullen waters
Of death's dark and silent sea!
Day by day I wait an answer,
But no answer comes to me.'

While she listened—vainly listened—
For some sound, though faint as sighs
Straight before her, slowly gliding,
Sailed two glistening dragon-flies
Bringing her the longed-for message
As if tidings from the skies;

L

For there flashed o'er memory's tablets
   A quick gleam from sudden rays,
Bringing back a German fable
   She had read in happier days,
Full of heavenly inspiration
   As a poet's worthiest lays.

Now the fable as narrated
   I shall here essay to tell,
With the hope that it may lighten
   Griefs like hers, and break the spell,
When in doubt some mourner questions,
   'With my lost ones is it well?'

FABLE OF THE DRAGON-FLY GRUBS.

There was a dark and sedgy pool,
   Where plants grew side by side;
Their roots were fast in mire below,
   Their tops swayed with the tide.

And here, low down on slimy bed,
   Some water creatures crept,
And thought their world a paradise,
   And groped, and ate, and slept.

No care disturbed their life's content,
 Save when some comrade dear
Climbed up a plant to fields of air,
 In them to disappear.

Then gathered they around the case
 Which once contained their kind ;
In solemn conclave sought of each
 The mystery to find.

' How can it be that he exists
 When this is thrown aside ?
Robbed of the form he once possessed,
 Where does he now abide ? '

Then said the eldest of them all,
 ' My turn will come to go,
And I shall find some way to tell
 What each one longs to know.'

The days passed on, and brought at last
 The hour he knew was near ;
And all his kinsfolk gathered round
 His promised words to hear.

He reached the top, he passed the edge
　Where stretched the ether plane ;
The case fell back, its inmate gone ;
　His comrades wait in vain.

No sound they heard, no sight they saw,
　Yet, flashing in the air,
Were iridescent wings of light
　Above them everywhere.

And he, the latest born of all,
　Close-skimmed the water's edge,
Peering far down the murky depths
　Amidst the swaying sedge.

He saw the groping forms below,
　The wistful glances sent,
As they looked upward from their home,
　To gain some tidings bent.

But all in vain he strove to tell,
　The mystery was o'er :
They cannot hear who grope in fear,
　*Not lost, but gone before.'

'Not my lost one!' said the mourner:
'Now I know thou waitest me
Beyond the brightening waters
Of death's solemn, silent sea;
And I wait the welcome message
Which will call me unto thee!'

STORIES FOR CHILDREN.

'KATIE DID:' A GOSSIP'S TALE.

Miss Magpie speaks.

'A GOOD MORNING, Madame Locust!
  Pray, have you heard the tale
About Miss Katie Green, the belle,
  Who lives in yonder vale?'

Mrs. Locust answers.

'Ah! no, indeed, Miss Maggie P.;
  I've not been out, you know;
And living up four pairs of stairs,
  I don't hear much below.
I hope the proud and pretty Kate
  Has not disgraced her name;
Her family are all well-bred,
  For from good blood they came.'

Miss Magpie.

'Well, Madame Locust, pride, you know,
  Is very unbecoming;

But though Kate Green's exceeding proud,
   She always was a-roaming,
And they do say she's very fast,
   And very wilful too;
And though I'm not at all a prude,
   Some things I'd never do.
And now they say she has eloped,
   With her own cousin too.
I don't believe all that I hear,
   But this I know is true,
For as I passed her mother's house
   I stopped beside the door,
And heard her sobbing " Katie did ;"
   I could not well hear more.'

Mrs. Locust.

' Why, that's a song they always sing
   When all the world is still :
I'm sure you must have heard them
   From every dale and hill.
I listen almost every night
   When in their homes they're hid,
Singing always the selfsame tune :
   The words are " Katie did."

I would not, then, repeat the tale,
  My friend, if I were you,
Until you have some better proof
  Of knowing it is true.'

The busy day passed round again,
  And evening, as before,
Found gossiping Miss Magpie
  At Neighbour Locust's door.

Miss Magpie.

'That story, Madame Locust,
  Is true as true can be;
For what's before one's own eyes
  One cannot help but see.
Dame Hornet lives just opposite
  Miss Katie's mother's door,
And I stepped in this afternoon:
  I never called before.
They're not counted in our set,
  Nor are they 'in the swim,'
But one must be agreeable
  When news one seeks to win.
So I found she knew her neighbours,
  And she talked for full an hour

About the Greens—how rich they were,
   And how they built a bower
Of emerald leaves and coral buds
   For Katie's use alone,
And to reward their kindness fond
   The wanton thing has flown.
And no one knows where she has gone.
   Her mother wept all day;
And when Mrs. Hornet asked her,
   One word she would not say.'

Mrs. Locust.

'Stop, stop, my friend! you talk too fast.
   I know where Kate has gone.
Look through my vine-clad window,
   And o'er yon verdant lawn.
You see that dwelling rich and chaste,
   As fair as e'er was seen?
That is the home of Katie now:
   Her name is *Mrs.* Green.
Her mother came around to-day
   To sit a while with me;
And when I found she felt so lone,
   I made her stay to tea.

Her Katie did not run away;
  She rode like any queen:
Two snow-white doves her coursers were,
  Her carriage gold and green,
A present from her loving lord
  Upon her bridal day.
Oh! that he is her cousin dear
  I quite forgot to say.
'Twas Katie's wish, her mother said,
  To have it kept so still;
There were no guests besides the Greens
  And Mrs. Whippoorwill.
But though her mother mourns her loss,
  I saw her eyes' deep light,
Which flashed so proudly when she told
  The splendours of that night—
The costly gifts his friends had brought
  To lavish on the bride;
And though she spoke with faltering tones,
  I saw her heartfelt pride.
So take a warning, Maggie Pye:
  With gossips don't be seen;
And if you hear some idle tale
  Remember Katie Green.

And don't give ear to slanders vile,
Much less the words repeat,
Or you will live to be despised
And scorned by those you meet.'

COWARDS.

HAROLD asks a story. What shall it be?
Of beautiful lands beyond the broad sea?
Or of fairies and gnomes in forests deep?
Or of soldiers who fight and women who weep?

'Tell me *all*, grandmamma—tell *all* to me;
Fairies and gnomes and lands beyond the sea.
First tell me, please, of the soldiers who fight;
If wrong for us boys, for men is it right?'

And Carl, standing by, opens wide his eyes,
Large, lovely and calm, and full of surprise:
'Can I fight, grandma, when I am a man?
Because I will wait until then, if I can.

'I would like to strike when Ulla looks grum
And sends me to bed for breaking my drum,
But I am so small and so short, you know,
I cannot reach up to give her a blow.'

'Oh, naughty Carl Diedrick! do you not know
They're cowards who strike a woman a blow?'
Cries Harold, looking severe as he can:
'But never a soldier, and never a man.'

DOGGEREL.

THREE little children waiting in a row,
Three little ponies saddled ' for to go,'
Three big chimney-sweeps stalking through the
    town,
The three frightened children all tumble down.

Three little ponies scampering one side,
Three little children much terrified ;
Three stalking chimney-sweeps full of delight,
Having occasioned the terrible fright.

Ten big Prussians going to the field,
Two little Frenchmen that will not yield ;
One mitrailleuse pouring out its fire,
Ten big Prussians marching on in ire.

Two little Frenchmen running like mad ;
The mitrailleuse which the Frenchmen had
Turned by the Prussians to fire on their foe ;
The two little Frenchmen don't know where to go.

Three big chimney-sweeps stalk all the night,
Trying to give other children a fright ;
Ten big Prussians following up their foe,
Two little Frenchmen still 'on the go.'

Three little ponies at a stable door,
Two little Frenchmen dying in their gore ;
Ten big Prussians flying to their king,
Who think they've done a wonderful thing.

Moral.

Though chimney-sweeps and bullies may some-
    times prevail,
We have not yet come to the end of the tale ;
The weak will grow strong, and the children some day
Will get to be men, and will go their own way.

When equal the numbers, a combat brings fame
To the victor who keeps untarnished his name.
Boys are bullies who press their much weaker foes,
And when they are fallen continue their blows.

Remember this, boys, when you've grown to be
    men—
Reinhold, Carl Clarence, and little Eugène ;
And if you should chance to have ever a foe,
When he is fallen don't strike him a blow.

THE BIRDS' NEST.

A Story for Eric.

' OH, mamma, I have seen the home
Of the robin and the wren ;
It was the dearest, sweetest spot
In all the wooded glen.

' The leaves were thickly hung around ;
You could not see the sky ;
And there, upon the shadiest bough,
They'd hung their nests so high.

' I could not reach, for all I tried
And stood upon my toes,
And thought to coax the black-eyed birds
By holding up my rose.

' It frightened them ; they left their nests,
And swiftly flew away ;
I trembled for the little birds,
And wanted them to stay.

M 2

' Then from behind a laurel bush
    I watched with eager view,
While, hopping back from bough to bough,
    The birdies' mammas flew.

' They snugged up to their little ones,
    And then I ran away ;
But may I not go back again
    To see their nests some day ? '

So little Edla asked mamma,
    And mamma said, ' My dear,
How would you like if giants came
    Within our cottage here?

' And if they frightened me away,
    How would you feel to see
The awful creatures standing near—
    As near as near could be? '

Then Edla shook her little head,
    With curls of sunny gold ;
And quickly answering, Edla said,
    ' The half could not be told

' Of all the fear that I should feel.
Even for birds 'tis true :
" Do unto others as you would
That others do to you." '

THE LITTLE TRUANT.

[ILLUSTRATION OF A PICTURE.]

' WHERE hast thou been, thou beautiful child ?
Wandering o'er hillsides, through woodlands wild,
Frightening the birds from the forest spray,
And gathering flowers by the shaded way ?
Why art thou standing in thoughtful mood ?
Is the brook too wanton, the breeze too rude ?
Or art thou wearied with idle play—
Wearied with rambling all the day ?'

' Afar through the vales where fountains flow,
And over the hills where violets grow,
And down in the meadows wide and green,
Where the lily droops its head unseen,
There have I wandered this lovely day·
With the humming bees and the birds to play.

' I fear to go to my mother mild ;
I know she has missed her truant child,

And, sadly grieved at my absence long,
She'll chide her darling for doing wrong ;
But oh, 'tis beautiful on the lea :
With the birds and flowers I love to be.

' I will take my buds to my mother dear,
And tell her for me she must never fear,
For I love the fresh and the sunny air,
The woodlands wild and the valleys fair ;
And God, who careth for bird and bee,
I am sure will always care for me.'

VOICES OF THE PAST.

MY COUNTRY.

WHAT shall I do for thee, my land,
  In this thy hour of need ?
Thy cry goes up unto the skies,
  And shall I take no heed ?

Shall all my nights be spent in rest,
  And all my days in ease,
While thousands sleep in tented fields
  Beneath the wintry breeze,

And thousands more by silent hearths
  Await the battle-cry ?
The keenest suffering in war
  Comes not to those who die.

O God ! to think of all the woe
  Beneath the mourner's roof,
The days of sickening, sad suspense
  That herald in the truth !

O God ! to think of all the tears
   That drench this hapless land
From Mississippi's winding course
   To broad Atlantic's strand !

Ah ! mothers, wives, and sisters fond
   Who wait the tidings dread,
I would our country might be saved,
   And you still weep no dead.

But did I count as many sons
   As did Cornelia bold,
I'd gird myself their weapons on,
   And speed them from my fold.

My eyes are full of gathering tears,
   But not for those away ;
Alas that I've not one to send
   To fight our cause to-day !

I'll give my time, my life, my all ;
   And may the offering be
As worthy of thee, O my land,
   As if I died for thee !

January 1864.

'*FORWARD, MARCH!*'

ON Newbern's bloody battle-ground,
   Bold as a crusade knight,
Our young lieutenant led us on,
   All eager for the fight.

' Forward, my men, my comrades brave !'
   His voice rang loud and clear ;
And, charging with our bayonets,
   We followed in the rear.

And, ever foremost, on he pressed ;
   Our ranks held firm and true,
Though volley after volley poured,
   And thinned us through and through.

' Well done, my boys ! the day is ours !
   Like veterans you've fought !'
Another crash of musketry :
   The day was dearly bought ;

For there upon the accursèd soil
　Our young lieutenant lay;
Too brave for even one low moan,
　His life-blood ebbed away.

Loud rang his voice, as clarion clear,
　As when he onward led :
' Forward, my boys ! the day is ours !'
　Then fell back with the dead.

And ' Forward !' is our battle-cry,
　Which through the land shall ring
Until the Union is restored
　And Liberty is king.

I.

IN ROME, MAY 1863.

NOT for Italy waking from fetters
  Of centuries' pestilent sleep,
Not for Italy arming for freedom,
  These tears of compassion I weep;
But my thoughts flow afar from this region,
  Afar from its classical lore,
My thoughts flow afar from this region,
  Back, back to my own native shore.
I mourn on the banks of the Tiber
  For the ills of my own native shore.

O Columbia! fairest of countries,
  Must thy valleys, so fruitful and still,
Be shorn, like these plains, of their glory,
  And yield to the conqueror's will?
Thy cities be swept of the treasures
  By peace and prosperity won,
Whilst the carnage of battle is raging
  'Twixt father and brother and son?

O Columbia! fairest of countries,
   Have the days of thy sorrow begun?

The days when the tears of thy orphans
   Shall sprinkle thy green sod like rain,
When countless the wives and the mothers
   Who mourn o'er their wounded and slain;
When the hopes of the nations in darkness,
   Whose eyes turned upon thee for light,
Shall grow faint in thy bitter despairing,
   Shall be lost in the blackness of night?
Alas for the hopes of the nations
   That trusted thy glory and might!

O Rome! in the days of thy glory,
   In the days of thy pomp and thy pride,
When thy legions outnumbered the nations
   Which thou in thy triumph defied,
Didst thou dream of the sad devastation
   That, hurtling o'er hillside and plain,
Should sweep down thy temples and columns
   As low as thy warriors slain?
Didst thou dream of the long night of silence
   That should fall o'er thy beautiful plain?

II.

AT HOME, MAY 1864.

THUS mused I in dark days of sadness
  Ere the purpose of God I had seen :
Our country was shattered and falling,
  No strength had it whereon to lean.
But now dawns its day of redemption,
  The time of its triumph draws nigh ;
No longer a nation of bondsmen
  Lift manacled hands to the sky ;
But God in His glory appeareth,
  And cleaving the channel of red
These dark hosts, by Him marshalled over,
  The fair land of promise shall tread ;
And the eyes of the nations in darkness
  Shall *still* turn upon us for light,
As, scaling the pure heights of freedom,
  We grow in our grandeur and might.

WIDOWED.

[ADMIRAL DU PONT DIED JUNE 30, 1865.]

TRUE to herself, to her heroic heart,
　Resigned she counts the hours that slowly glide,
As when her country called, though loth to part,
　She braved the days that kept him from her side.

Ah! those were times of troubled, wearing fear,
　But through the murderous storms of shot and
　　shell
He lived to count his victory complete,
　And meet the homage he had earned so well.

' Waiting for orders,' to his home he sped.
　Ah, God be praised! the orders never came,
And months slipped by in joy and solace rare,
　Save that the land he loved was scourged by
　　flame—

Save that unto his judgment and his skill,
    Ripened by rich experience of years,
They paid no heed, but wrought the weaker will,
    While Time made manifest how just his fears;

How wise and true, counsels that might have saved
    An untold number of most precious lives,
Uncounted sums of treasure to our land,
    And myriad tears of mothers, sisters, wives!

'Waiting for orders!'   Suddenly they came,
    But not to marshal hosts as erst before;
Not into danger's midst God calls him now,
    But through the portals of His golden door.

His perfect life, rounded with duties filled,
    Closed on him calmly as a summer's day;
No shock of pain, no anguished gaze of love,
    Wrestled in vain to bid his spirit stay.

The scathing flame had cleansed his country free,
    And holy Peace was brooding o'er the land;
A fitting time for one to pass from earth
    Whose days have left us such a record grand.

But for the anguish of his widowed one
We may not check unbidden tears that flow;
Comfort her with Thy presence, O our Christ!
And give her peace such as God's angels know.

OUR HERO.

ULYSSES S. GRANT.

As some great Sphinx looms up before the sight,
To travellers crossing o'er the Libyan sands,
Calm and majestic in its grand repose
As are the chiselled saints of Christian lands ;
So, in the future, will his name bring up
To those who tread the golden sands of life,
His deeds heroic in our time of need—
His greatness when had closed the days of strife.
And, like that Sphinx with face serene and calm,
Those deeds, this greatness, shall for ever stand,
Kindling the hearts of nations yet unborn—
Thrilling the noble souls of every land !

THE SEASONS.

AN APRIL DAY.

THE April rain falls slowly,
  Like tears that follow sighs,
And fleecy clouds glide lightly
  Over the azure skies;
The soft south wind is wooing
  The pale clematis vine,
Dallying with its tendrils
  As trustingly they twine.

The east a rainbow spanneth,
  Promise of watchful care—
A glowing, gorgeous banner,
  That fairies might prepare
With rays of gold and purple,
  With emeralds' flashing light,
With tints from deep blue sapphires,
  And hearts of rubies bright.

From sward that spreads before me
  The crocus lifts its head,
And pale and starry flowers
  Peep from their winter bed;
And o'er the latticed trellis
  The clinging vine doth creep,
While down amid the mossy turf
  The harebell lies asleep.

I love the gentle April—
  Her soft and balmy sighs;
Her smiles are ofttimes tearful,
  But hope's in her earnest eyes;
Sweet in truth is the lesson
  That grief may learn alway,
For, ever, weeping April
  Is followed by joyous May.

A DAY IN MIDSUMMER.

Lo! from yonder rising upland
　　Springs the dewy-footed Morn,
Sweeping with her waving garments
　　Through the fields of rustling corn.
Through the vale she swiftly glideth,
　　Breathing on the billowy grain,
And, like amber wavelets flowing,
　　See it sparkle o'er the plain.

Now she bends beside the fountain
　　In the deep and dark ravine,
Bathes her lips and sunny forehead,
　　Wreathes her brow with garlands green.
In the grand old woods she wanders,
　　Through the blossoming leafy bowers,
Weaving in a perfumed chaplet
　　Tender buds and sweetest flowers.

To the lightly-dancing streamlet
  Breatheth she sweet notes of glee
As adown the rocks it leapeth,
  Laughing o'er the level lea.
In her eyes you see no traces
  Of the depths of natal gloom
Which her parent, Night, enshrouded,
  As she weeping left his tomb.

Light of heart, she onward hastens,
  Humming o'er the water's tune,
While, upon the hill-tops sleeping,
  Waits her younger sister, Noon.
Morn awakes her with her kisses,
  And the beauty lifts her eyes
On the sunny vales and uplands
  Where the grass enamelled lies.

Flinging back her golden tresses,
  Waving in voluptuous light,
Now the graceful Noon arises,
  Glorious in her sister's sight.
Then the maiden Morn departeth,
  And sweet Noon walks forth alone,
Languishing beside the fountains
  For her lovely sister flown.

Every hour she grows still sadder,
   Every hour she mourns in vain,
Till at length the star-crowned Evening
   Hastens o'er the lonely plain;
Struck with wonder at the beauty
   Even of her fading charms,
Evening bows entranced before her,
   And she sleeps within his arms.

AUTUMN SCENES.

AUTUMN is here. His russet mantle's fold
   Trails over all the woodland groves around,
Scattering bright gems of purple set in gold
   Like drifts of amethysts to the mossy ground.
The katydid has ceased her plaintive tale,
   The whippoorwill has sought a southern zone,
Alone the corn-bird calls along the vale,
   And listens to the hoarse wind's answering tone.

The grass-grown path beside the chestnut wood
   Is nearly hidden by the drifting leaves ;
The plough-boy gleans the nuts where thickest
      strewed,
   Or helps the farmer stack his yellow sheaves ;
The river, murmuring o'er its rocky bed,
   Smiles up as fondly to the forest spray
As if it sought the falling leaves to wed,
   And bear them from their sheltered home away.

The wild flower, shivering on its slender stalk,
  Meets the rude blast, and sways to rise again,
Spreading its petals gay by woodland walk,
  Heedless of drenching dews and beating rain.
Not so its sister plants in garden bowers;
  They droop and die, afraid of winter's cold,
All save the artemisia's clustering flowers,
  The dahlia and the stately marigold.

'Midst all of autumn's ever mournful sounds
  The cricket chirps his never-ceasing lay,
And wild bees, buzzing o'er their daily rounds,
  Hasten to bear their stolen sweets away.
The labourer, plodding homeward from his toil
  O'er fields where gleaners gathered all the day,
Finds a few scattered sheaves upon the soil,
  And with a light heart whistles on his way.

Once in his home, his cheerful wife will meet
  With welcoming smiles his true and fond caress;
His little ones will gather round his feet,
  And humble happiness his hours will bless.
Ah! praised be God for all the garnered love
  That makes our earthly pilgrimage so bright,
Leading our thoughts to mansions fair above,
  Where never falls the darkness of the night.

WINTER.

THE tattered robes of autumn cling
  Around the trembling forest trees,
Falling at touch of wild bird's wing
  Or sighing of the troubled breeze.
The gorgeous beauty of her prime
  Has faded from the woods away ;
A stranger from an arctic clime
  Woos the sad earth by night and day

He hangs her brow with jewels rare,
  He wraps her form in ermine white,
And gems a queen might deign to wear
  Gleam, from its folds, prismatic light.
In vain is all the wealth he brings ;
  She sadly sighs for days agone,
For autumn's bright and beauteous things,
  For summer's laughing, joyous tone.

At his embrace her heart grows chill ;
　She shudders as he clasps her round ;
The pulses of her life stand still,
　A bride reluctant he has found.
Alas! she mourneth not alone
　The hours that are for ever past,
The happy days for ever flown,
　Too brightly beautiful to last.

I know of eyes now dim with tears,
　I know of breasts grown strangely cold,
For wintry smiles and questioning fears
　Have changed those loving eyes of old.
Oh, would that Summer in the heart
　Might ever hold her gentle reign,
Or if stern Winter claims a part
　She would resume her sway again.

But no.　Unlike the changing years,
　When once her radiant form has flown
In vain you woo her smiles or tears,
　In vain the living dead you mourn.
Ah ! cherish, then, your summer days,
　Your autumn glories, as they fly ;
Too soon will come the wintry rays
　When all their beauties fade and die.

O

SONNETS.

I.

MORNING.

THE morning breaks. Across the amber sky
Grey clouds are trooping slowly one by one,
Their edges crimsoned by the rising sun.
   Mist wreaths upon the distant mountains lie,
And violet vapours through the valley glide,
   Veiling the crystal stream that winds along,
   For ever murmuring, in low, gushing song,
To the sweet flowers and fern that droop beside.
   My heart to God springs up in thankful prayer !
Most beautiful on such a morn doth seem
This earth; most radiant, as the sun's first gleam
   Flashes afar athwart the woodland fair.
In pleasant ways my pilgrimage is cast :
God only grant these happy days may last!

II.

NOON.

THE glorious sun is midway in the sky,
But for the clouds it scarcely can be seen ;
Their shadows fall across the meadows green,
    And o'er the brown fields where the sheaves
    still lie.
Ah ! now my heart is filled with boding dread,
    And tears break slowly from my downcast eyes
    Like drops of rain from all unwilling skies,
When April's flowers bloom fair above the dead.
    A whisper trembles through the noontide air;
The rustling of the pines the wind before,
Mayhap, yet sounds a dirge like 'nevermore.'
    And back I gaze upon the past so fair,
Yet glean not courage for the coming night,
From whence I see no ray of guiding light !

III.

NIGHT.

TO-NIGHT a thick mist fills the valley wide,
And banks of clouds wall in the arching skies,
Hiding the starlight from my wistful eyes.
Black loom the rocks upon the dark hill-side,
And all is drear and lone, where late, so gay,
The reapers toiled amid the golden grain,
Leaving the ripened field with loaded wain,
To wait the dawning of another day.
O gloomy night! thy shadows fall on me,
As in the shrouded future I divine
Still darker hours than ever yet were mine.
Then o'er my breast the waves of sorrow's sea
Shall beat more fiercely for the calm before.
Ah, Life! how wild the storms that sweep thy
shore!

ERAS IN LIFE.

FOREBODINGS.

'An imminence of something unknown is felt.'
'Forebodings come, we know not how or whence,
Shadowing a nameless fear upon the soul.'—Miss Procter.

WHAT weight is this which presses on my soul ?
 Powerless to rise, I sink upon the dust ;
The days in solemn cycle o'er me roll,
 While, praying, I can only wait and trust ;

Trust the dear Hand that all my life has led
 Through pastures green, by waters pure and still ;
· If now He leads me through dark ways, and
  dread,
 Shall I dare murmur, whatso'er His will ?

Give me, dear Lord, the strength I so much
  need—
 Do Thou but guide through earth-defiling ways,
Then will I follow where Thy hand doth lead,
 With feet unfaltering in my darkest days.

December 1872.

THORNS AND ARROWS.

ONE day I made complaint because some thorns
Had pierced me when I stooped to find a flower,
Forgetting no rose bloomed without such dower
Down the long years of fair and dewy morns.

Another time I wept some bitter tears
In that from pleasant pastures I had strayed,
While in a labyrinth my way was laid,
Which seemed as endless as the untold years.

Once more I made lament ; and that was when
A creature, bright with many-coloured hues,
Which fearful I the thing its life would lose
Had rescued from the slime of bog and fen,

In which it struggling lay, and gasped for breath ;
And when in safety on my hearth 'twas laid,
I fed it from my hand, nor felt afraid
That it would turn and sting me to my death.

But all in vain my simple trust had birth :
The creature struck its fangs against my heart ;
Save that it found no vulnerable part, ˙
I now would be but as a clod of earth.

There came an hour in which I made no moan,
But sat apart from morn to eve, nor wept,
And through long laggard nights my watch I
    kept,
With heart more heavy than the quarried stone.

Then said I, ' Sage and seer are true who write
That little troubles most our lives will fret,
And pierce the heart with poison-fanged regret,
And loudest make lament by day and night.

' But when some mortal anguish smites its blow,
The sore heart hides its pain from searching eyes,
Stifles each moan and checks the telltale sighs
That would reveal the torture of its woe.'

And then I prayed : ' O God, for ever just !
Forgive me that I made such loud complaint
O'er ills that every human life must taint,
Till the immortal rends its robe of dust.

' But now, dear Lord, Thou knowest all my grief,
Thou seest how my heart is drenched in blood,
And how my tears surge in a prisoned flood
That, pent within my breast, brings no relief.

' Canst Thou not draw the arrow from my heart
And stay the bleeding ere my life flows out ? '
Why should I ask or let one wretched doubt
Within my questioning soul have place or part ?

He sees my woe, He knows its bitter cause ;
He weighs my heart, He counts my prisoned tears
And all my dead hopes shrouded on their biers ;
And when His time arrives, He will not pause,

But draw the arrow if its work be o'er,
And close the wound until it leaves no scar,
And raise the dead from sepulchres ajar,
And, born anew, my hopes and joys restore.

MY GETHSEMANE.

ALL night I wept and prayed, and prayed and
  wept,
  But when the morning came the pain was there;
I could not drown my sorrow with my tears,
  Nor could I lose it in long hours of prayer.
Then to my memory came a holy spot
  Where once I knelt in a far eastern land,—
The cave where Christ withdrew within the mount,
  Leaving in sleep's soft arms his cherished band.
The votive lamps burned low before the shrine,
  Where flowers heaped in loving offerings lay,
And costly incense heavy made the air,
  While pilgrims knelt from morn till eve to pray.
Here had my Saviour wrestled with His soul,
  While drops like blood streamed down His pallid
    face;
Here had the angel ministered to Him:
  Here had His heart been filled with heavenly
    grace.

But not from Him the bitter cup did pass :
An angel held it while He drank its lees.
Dear God, must I too drain this bitter cup,
In my Gethsemane, on bended knees ?
Ah ! here I'll wait Thy angel, for I know
No soul is left to struggle on alone :
Sooner or later comes the strength we ask,
Sooner or later are our sorrows flown.

'O GOD, BE PITIFUL!'

TEMPTATION TO DOUBT GOD'S PROVIDENCE AND RESISTANCE
TO HIS WILL.

AGAINST a wall of rock my helpless hands
Beat with the fierceness of despairing force ;
The darkness settles round, and not one ray
Pierces the deadly gloom where late the sun
Sprinkled its light and warmth in golden showers.
I thought the earth so grandly beautiful,
The universe but made for sweetest joys,
And now where is the beauty, where the joy ?
I fold my weak, bruised hands across my heart,
And from its depths my soul sends forth the cry,
' O God, be pitiful !'   And still the rocks
Loom high, and still the darkness ever grows,
And neither God nor man is pitiful.

What knowest thou of God, complaining soul,
That thou shouldst dare to doubt His pitying love ?

P

If, wandering from the paths in which thy feet
Were set, thou strayest into darkness blank
And fall against the rocks that keep us well
Within their bounds, rather give thanks to Him
Who stretched the barrier for our good, to save
Our feet from farther straying.   God not pitiful!
Recall the impious thought, and ne'er forget
That no soul cries in vain, ' Be pitiful, O God!'

'*BE BRAVE!*'

BE brave! poor heart, be brave!
And suffer and grow strong!
Just when the night the darkest is
The day will break ere long.

Be brave! sad heart, be brave!
And falter not nor fear:
For when the road the longest seems
The turning-point is near!

Be brave! strong heart, be brave!
These words say o'er and o'er,
Until the *pulse* has ceased to beat,
And lips can plead no more!

SUBMISSION.

I KNEW not Thou didst close and seal
The fountains in my pilgrim life—
That I should traverse arid plains,
Encountering Bedouin strife.

I knew not it was Thou, or else
I would not so have murmured, Lord,
To find my gushing fountains sealed,
My palm-trees fallen on the sward.

I knew not whence the arrows flew
That tore my bleeding heart in twain ;
For had I known Thine was the mark,
I could have borne the torturing pain.

I knew not that Thy guiding love
Decreed from idols, I had made,
I must be torn to do Thy will :
And knowing not, I was afraid.

But now I see that it is Thou,
Welcome the loss, the pain, the strife ;
For whatsoever is Thy will
Shall always be my will in life.

EVIL AND GOOD.

'The soul of good in things evil.'—STOPFORD BROOKE.
'A sublime feeling of a presence comes about me at times.'
F. W. ROBERTSON.

IN the lap of the mountains I lie,
Looking up to the cloudland of sky,
While a vision, keen, piercing, and clear,
Descends from the gods to me here,
Till I see the pale spirits *flit* by.

What mission have they to fulfil?
And is it of good or of ill?
No answer from far or from near;
And trustful I rest without fear,
And wait as before on God's will.

I hear not a breath nor a sigh,
Yet some power for ever is nigh:
Some Presence beside me keeps guard,
Around me to watch and to ward,
And evil for ever must fly.

Yet evil clings close to the good,
As the rough bark clings to the wood;
And evil its course must perform
Through sorrow and darkness and storm,
Through fire of trial withstood.

And good with the evil must grow:
In the field where white lilies blow
Bloom the blood-red blossoms of sin:
We know not how deeply within
Strikes their stain on bosoms of snow.

But the stain, the sin and the pain,
And the grief, is never in vain:
We suffer, endure, and grow strong,
And our right is born of our wrong;
And through fire our gold we regain!

SAN MORITZ: *August* 1879.

WRECKED.

WEIRD was the face of the ocean,
  Wild was the pitiless blast,
As driven before it madly
  A vessel's wreck swept past.

Out of the gaping port-holes
  Poured seas of foaming brine ;
From battered hulk to broken masts
  No living thing made sign.

Straightway in dreams before me
  My own wrecked life passed by—
When I was left on seas of grief
  To sink with no help nigh.

But He who holds the ocean
  In hollow of His hand
Guided that vessel into port
  And brought me to the land.

The stanch ship, stored with treasure
  Of silver and of gold,
Held all confided to its care
  Safe in its iron hold.

My barque, though wrecked, deserted,
  Holds now its treasure still,
And He who brought it into port
  Does with it as He will.

DEAD HOPES.

I HAVE left my life behind me,
I have buried my past to-day,
And turned the lock of the grave-yard
    And given the key away.

I know will come days of longing—
O days of unspeakable dread !—
When I shall go back in spirit
    To look on my precious dead.

But I shall not faint nor falter,
Nor show by a word nor a sign,
How I mourn for what lies buried
    In this grave-yard heart of mine.

And they who know not my anguish,
My woe, and its deathless pain,
Will smile with kind words of greeting,
    Counting my loss as my gain.

Their smiles with smiles I will answer,
For they shall not read in my face
How I mourn my dead hopes buried,
    How I watch the sacred place.

Whate'er befalls in the future,
Life's lessons have taught me to say,—
' The Lord directeth the steps of man,
    Though his heart devise the way.'

WAITING.

OVER the sea, over the sea, eyes of mine look
    wistfully :
Day follows night, and night follows day,
And night and day are one alway,
As over the sea, over the sea, eyes of mine look
    wistfully.

Over the sea, over the sea, eyes of mine look
    earnestly :
I see no isle, I see no shore,
I only hear the billows roar,
As over the sea, over the sea, eyes of mine look
    earnestly.

Over the sea, over the sea, eyes of mine look
    dreamily :
I soon will hear the pilot's call,
With sound of oars that rise and fall,
As over the sea, over the sea, eyes of mine look
    dreamily.

Over the sea, over the sea, eyes of mine look
    fearlessly :
The pilot Death is near at hand,
He steers his bark unto this strand,
As over the sea, over the sea, eyes of mine look
    fearlessly.

Over the sea, over the sea, eyes of mine look
    eagerly :
I see the gold and jasper gate,
I see the angels watch and wait,
As over the sea, over the sea, eyes of mine look
    eagerly.

Over the sea, over the sea, eyes of mine look
    tenderly :
I see the faces gone before
Watching for me at heaven's door ;
Over the sea, over the sea, take me, pilot, tenderly !

MEMORIAL.

'OH, tell me, are the fields of heaven
  As fair as earth's are now,
With all their wealth of living green
  And roseate bloom of bough?

'I think when frosts of autumn come
  And leaves grow brown and sere,
The fading of the flowers would make
  E'en heaven more fair appear.'

The autumn came, with gorgeous wealth
  Of opalescent glow;
She faded with the fading leaf,
  Before the winter's snow.

The spring's soft green, the summer's bloom,
  The autumn's drifts of gold,
Are now as nought to one who walks
  In fairer scenes untold.

But they who loved her miss her most
When spring's first blossoms blow,
And when the leaves of autumn burn
With red and golden glow.

For always doth the spring recall
Her lingering love of earth,
And autumn brings the memory
Of her immortal birth.

THE MINISTERING SPIRIT.

FOUR gates there are that open into heaven :
The first of deep-hued amethyst, fold on fold ;
The second, jacinth is ; the third of pearl ;
The fourth, of inwrought work of jewelled gold.

The amethyst gate they only enter in
In whom both 'faith and charity' abound ;
Good works' the jacinth ; 'pure of heart' the pearl ;
The fourth, they who were tried, nor wanting
found.

Weary of earth, heart-sore and faint, there came
A pilgrim spirit to the purple gate :
Its violet folds were closed, and opened not
To give one glimpse of heaven's celestial state.

On to the jacinth gate the traveller went :
Its amber crystal rose like wall of glass,
Nor open swung at her imploring cry,
Within to let the weary wanderer pass.

The gate of pearl, with prism-glowing tints,
 Feebly she next with faltering hands essayed;
A message came: 'Pass to the golden gate!
 Our King awaits thee there. Be not afraid!'

Emboldened thus, the woman hastened on:
 The gate flew open; throngs on either side
Welcomed with amaranth wreaths and sound of
  harps
 As forth to meet her came 'The Crucified.'

Within the jewelled gate the pilgrim passed,
 Led by her Lord, transfigured like to Him,
While wave on wave of music flowed through
  heaven
 From chanting, wingèd hosts of seraphim.

Amazed, the earth-born to her Saviour said,
 'What wrought I, Lord, for Thy dear name on
  earth,
That Thou shouldst meet *me* at the gate of gold—
 Accused, reviled, my good name robbed of
  worth?'

Q

'Living for others, thou hast lived for Me;
 Conquering thyself, the conqueror's crown is
 given:
Faithful in all committed to thy care,
 Hath brought thee through the golden gate to
 heaven.'

And now, no longer weary nor heart-sore,
 This pilgrim spirit works for mortals still;
No longer fettered by earth's fears and cares,
 But free as angels are to do God's will.

Now, to the wayworn on this planet left,
 On viewless pinions borne, she comes and goes;
They know not whence the calm sustaining strength
 That to them ofttimes like a river flows!

Ah, messengers there are from heaven to earth,
 In these our days, as in the days of old:
And those sent back to strengthen and console
 Are they who enter by the gate of gold!

LONDON : PRINTED BY
SPOTTISWOODE AND CO., NEW-STREET SQUARE
AND PARLIAMENT STREET

Errata.

Page 6, 1st line, *read* 'I am no coward,' were the words she said,
,,   20, 3rd line, 3rd verse, *read* I shall know it's but fancy for me,
,,   26, 2nd line, 4th verse, *read* Where, far beyond the asphodel,
,,   47, *for* title Resignation, *read* Recompense.
,,   81, last line but one, *read* When Ambition's torch still lured me,
,, 108, 3rd line, 2nd verse, *read* Like that we find in hours of prayer
,, ,, last verse, 1st line, *read* My every grief to Thee I'll take,
,, 125, last verse, 2nd line, *read* Calling for others their full ranks to swell?
,, 129, last line, 3rd verse, *read* E'en if to learn them I myself must die.
,, 135, 2nd verse, last line but one, *read* See no sign by which you know
,, 211, 3rd verse, 3rd line, *read* Until the pulse has ceased to beat,

---

'The verses sing themselves.'—Rev. W. H. FURNESS, D.D.

'These songs were first sung to the author's circle of friends, and she has at last yielded to the wishes of those who saw more merit in her little hearth-sung lyrics than she has seen. . . . "Blossoms and Thorns" is a psalm of sorrow which makes us think that our night-bird sings with her heart against a thorn. Its burden is, that the perfect bliss of heaven can be won only through earthly trial, and it is a most forcible and felicitous pronunciation of that divine truth.'—SUNDAY MERCURY.

'Living for others, thou hast lived for Me;
  Conquering thyself, the conqueror's crown is
    given:
Faithful in all committed to thy care,

In these our days, as in the days of old:
And those sent back to strengthen and console
Are they who enter by the gate of gold!

LONDON : PRINTED BY
SPOTTISWOODE AND CO., NEW-STREET SQUARE
AND PARLIAMENT STREET

'This author, whose modest motto is,

> "Disdain us not, O kindly heart of man !
> Us unregarded poets of the earth,
> The little songsters, singing as we can,
> Our eager melodies of little worth,"

is wholly the reverse of transcendental. She puts her mind upon the page, expressing her thoughts in the plainest language; and because, as Campbell said,

> "Song is but the eloquence of Truth,"

the result is—poetry. . . . To justify our opinion we quote the poem "Grandchildren," which, in its tender naturalness, has rarely been surpassed.'—PHILADELPHIA PRESS.

'It is the naturalness of the lyrics that pleases—the difference between a living spring of pure water and the fluid served from a hydrant.'—Dr. R. SHELTON MACKENZIE.

'The verses sing themselves.'—Rev. W. H. FURNESS, D.D.

'These songs were first sung to the author's circle of friends, and she has at last yielded to the wishes of those who saw more merit in her little hearth-sung lyrics than she has seen. . . . "Blossoms and Thorns" is a psalm of sorrow which makes us think that our night-bird sings with her heart against a thorn. Its burden is, that the perfect bliss of heaven can be won only through earthly trial, and it is a most forcible and felicitous pronunciation of that divine truth.'—SUNDAY MERCURY.

'As an example of a poem nearly erfect in its way, we instance here "Love's Four Seasons." It is difficult to point out how the poem could be better. We might say the same of numerous others. Perhaps, for a more extended poem, "The Warden's Tale " is the best in the book. Some of the poems rise into a passionate earnestness that, in these conventional days, we had thought had come to be almost forgotten. Of these, "Gethsemane " is particularly noticeable. There are some stories for children, in rhyme, which are excellent.'--PETERSON'S MAGAZINE.

'This volume is the expression of a tender, true, womanly soul; varied, passionate, patriotic, and devotional. . . . The language is forcible and elegant, the rhythm melodious. . . . But her poetry is not mere harmony of words nor choiceness of diction. It bears the true inspiration.'—CHICAGO TIMES.

'This author is not only a poet, but one of the most refined and elevated type. "Blossoms and Thorns" and "Compensation" are gems. "A Battle Cry" has the sound of a silver trumpet; it is the cry of a brave, exultant heart, that fears neither slander nor envy. "The Warden's Tale" is the finest poem that has appeared for a long time.'—CHICAGO EVENING JOURNAL.

' "The Warden's Tale," "Love's Four Seasons." No one has ever written anything upon these subjects more perfect in thought and form. Were these poems known beyond the author's limited circle of friends, they would live as long as the English language lives. The charm of them is that they are human, not angelic. They describe with passionate earnestness the passionate feelings of a human heart, and this it is which makes them strong and great.'
CORⱢ OF LONDON STANDARD.

'One of the strongest poems of the series is "Temptation and Resistance," and indicates beyond doubt the author's radiant confidence, "That no soul cries in vain, ' Be pitiful, O God ! '" It is this faith in the unbounded love and mercy of God that moulds and shapes this author's course of thought, be it expressed either in prose or verse. The natural consequence is that her works are earnest and helpful from beginning to end. Her poems are still farther characterised by a sweet and generous sympathy with human suffering and affliction. A noble purpose runs through all this author's works, and we doubt if any one can read them without being the better for it. . . . Some of her songs are exquisite, and entitle her to an enviable place among New England poets. We speak of her as a New Englander, for though a resident of Philadelphia she really belongs to Massachusetts. Among her ancestral connections are some of the brightest names of the Colonial and Revolutionary days. It would be strange, then, if her writings were not saturated with thoroughly religious purpose and sentiment.'—HARTFORD EVENING POST.

'That most perfect poem, "The Warden's Tale," is the best and most delicate interpretation of temptation and erratic passion I have ever read.'—Rev. E. N. J. P.

'If poetry really is the highest expression of sentiment and feeling, then does this author often rise to the sublimest heights of literature. That she is one who feels deeply, thinks profoundly, and is animated by only the purest and most elevated sentiments, is made apparent upon every page of the volume. Not all that she has written, but much of it, must live in our literature, and live to adorn it. . . . She is one of the sweetest of the singers of to-day. She writes from within, and hence the hold that her poems take upon the feelings of others. . . . "Blossoms and Thorns," "The Soul's Citadel," "My Gethsemane," and "The Stranger," we enumerate as expressing a feeling of religious zeal and fervour half divine, and a faith which is all-sufficient to itself. The volume has, by its inherent merits, commanded not only the recognition, but the hearty commendation of the most severely critical minds, who have welcomed this author as a genuine poet, whose songs are sweet, graceful, and tender.'—PHILADELPHIA INQUIRER.

'The author of "On Dangerous Ground" seems to possess qualities as a poet which even surpass those which she has displayed in her prose writings. She evinces a fine poetic insight, a delicate appreciation of all the demands of rhythm, harmony, melody, and whatever goes in poetry to the proper outward surroundings of the poetic thought and inspiration. There are no faults in the mechanism of her lines to jar on the susceptible ear, or to offend the fastidious taste; but their music is sweet and strong, and often grand, and the correspondence between the theme and its setting is frequently so perfect as to constitute the highest attainment in poetic art. Then there is a spontaneity about her verses which carries the conviction of earnestness and truth, and, in short, impresses the reader with the feeling that this poet does not sing for the sake of hearing herself, but that she, like Tennyson, might say,

> "I do but sing because I *must*,
> And pipe but as the linnets sing."

We find in this volume much which is earnest, honest, true, and therefore strong and effective. The graces are not lacking, and they are fortified by that deep conviction and truth which saves them from any charge of weakness, and which makes us respect while we admire.'—BRIDGEPORT STANDARD.

'Not a few of the poems evince genius; and some, especially "The Warden's Tale," have a rare beauty of expression, and teach important lessons.'—NORTHAMPTON JOURNAL.

'The poems display much genius and taste.'
GREENFIELD GAZETTE.

'Writing graceful verses is this author's forte. A large portion of her poems evidently came out of the depths of a touching experience of life's joys and sorrows. . . . We are particularly impressed with such pieces as "Wheat and Chaff" (My heart lay on the threshing floor), "A Picture" (Only a churchyard covered with snow), "An Answer," &c., &c., and finally and emphatically would we instance, as among the happiest specimens of the author's simple grace, fluency, and beauty, "A Day in Midsummer" and "Love and Fame; an Allegory." '—BOSTON TRANSCRIPT.

'The poems display great poetical ability and a cultivated taste.'
SPRINGFIELD UNION.

A LIST OF

C. KEGAN PAUL AND CO.'S
PUBLICATIONS.

A LIST OF

C. KEGAN PAUL AND CO.'S PUBLICATIONS.

ADAMS (F. O.), F.R.G.S.

The History of Japan. From the Earliest Period to the Present Time. New Edition, revised. 2 volumes. With Maps and Plans. Demy 8vo. Cloth, price 21s. each.

ADAMS (W. D.).

Lyrics of Love, from Shakespeare to Tennyson. Selected and arranged by. Fcap. 8vo. Cloth extra, gilt edges, price 3s. 6d.

Also, a Cheap Edition. Fcap. 8vo. Cloth, price 2s. 6d.

ADAMSON H. T.), B.D.

The Truth as it is in Jesus. Crown 8vo. Cloth, price 8s. 6d.

The Three Sevens. Crown 8vo. Cloth, price 5s. 6d.

A. K. H. B.

From a Quiet Place. A New Volume of Sermons. Crown 8vo. Cloth, price 5s.

ALBERT (Mary).

Holland and her Heroes to the year 1585. An Adaptation from Motley's " Rise of the Dutch Republic." Small crown 8vo. Cloth, price, 4s. 6d.

ALLEN (Rev. R.), M.A.

Abraham; his Life, Times, and Travels, 3,800 years ago. Second Edition. With Map. Post 8vo. Cloth, price 6s.

ALLEN (Grant), B.A.

Physiological Æsthetics. Large post 8vo. 9s.

ALLIES (T. W.), M.A.

Per Crucem ad Lucem. The Result of a Life. 2 vols. Demy 8vo. Cloth, price 25s.

A Life's Decision. Crown 8vo. Cloth, price 7s. 6d.

AMATEUR.

A Few Lyrics. Small crown 8vo. Cloth, price 2s.

ANDERSON (Col. R. P.).

Victories and Defeats. An Attempt to explain the Causes which have led to them. An Officer's Manual. Demy 8vo. Cloth, price 14s.

ANDERSON (R. C.), C.E.

Tables for Facilitating the Calculation of every Detail in connection with Earthen and Masonry Dams. Royal 8vo. Cloth, price £2 2s.

Antiope. A Tragedy. Large crown 8vo. Cloth, price 6s.

ARCHER (Thomas).

About my Father's Business. Work amidst the Sick, the Sad, and the Sorrowing. Crown 8vo. Cloth, price 2s. 6d.

Army of the North German Confederation.

A Brief Description of its Organization, of the Different Branches of the Service and their rôle in War, of its Mode of Fighting, &c. &c. Translated from the Corrected Edition, by permission of the Author, by Colonel Edward Newdigate. Demy 8vo. Cloth, price 5s.

ARNOLD (Arthur).

Social Politics. Demy 8vo. Cloth, price 14s.

Free Land. Crown 8vo. Cloth, price 6s.

AUBERTIN (J. J.).

Camoens' Lusiads. Portuguese Text, with Translation by. With Map and Portraits. 2 vols. Demy 8vo. Price 30s.

AUBERTIN (J. J.).—*continued.*

Seventy Sonnets of Ca-
moens'. Portuguese text and translation, with some original poems.
Dedicated to Captain Richard F.
Burton. Printed on hand-made paper.
Cloth, bevelled boards, gilt tops,
price 7*s. 6d.*

Aunt Mary's Bran Pie.
By the author of "St. Olave's."
Illustrated. Cloth, price 3*s. 6d.*

AVIA.

The Odyssey of Homer
Done into English Verse. Fcap.
4to. Cloth, price 15*s.*

BADGER (George Perry), D.C.L.

An English-Arabic Lexi-
con. In which the equivalents for
English words and idiomatic sentences are rendered into literary and
colloquial Arabic. Royal 4to. Cloth,
price £9 9*s.*

BAGEHOT (Walter).

Some Articles on the De-
preciation of Silver, and Topics
connected with it. Demy 8vo. Price
5*s.*

The English Constitution.
A New Edition, Revised and
Corrected, with an Introductory
Dissertation on Recent Changes and
Events. Crown 8vo. Cloth, price
7*s. 6d.*

Lombard Street. A
Description of the Money Market.
Seventh Edition. Crown 8vo. Cloth,
price 7*s. 6d.*

BAGOT (Alan).

Accidents in Mines : their
Causes and Prevention. Crown 8vo.
Cloth, price 6*s.*

BAKER (Sir Sherston, Bart.).

Halleck's International
Law ; or Rules Regulating the
Intercourse of States in Peace and
War. A New Edition, Revised, with
Notes and Cases. 2 vols. Demy
8vo. Cloth, price 38*s.*

The Laws relating to Qua-
rantine. Crown 8vo. Cloth, price
12*s. 6d.*

BALDWIN (Capt. J. H.), F.Z.S.

The Large and Small Game
of Bengal and the North-West-
ern Provinces of India. 4to. With
numerous Illustrations. Second Edition. Cloth, price 21*s.*

BANKS (Mrs. G. L.).

God's Providence House.
New Edition. Crown 8vo. Cloth,
price 3*s. 6d.*

Ripples and Breakers.
Poems. Square 8vo. Cloth, price 5*s.*

BARLEE (Ellen).

Locked Out : a Tale of the
Strike. With a Frontispiece. Royal
16mo. Cloth, price 1*s. 6d.*

BARNES (William).

An Outline of English
Speechcraft. Crown 8vo. Cloth,
price 4*s.*

Poems of Rural Life, in the
Dorset Dialect. New Edition,
complete in 1 vol. Crown 8vo. Cloth,
price 8*s. 6d.*

Outlines of Redecraft
(Logic). With English Wording.
Crown 8vo. Cloth, price 3*s.*

BARTLEY (George C. T.).

Domestic Economy : Thrift
in Every Day Life. Taught in
Dialogues suitable for Children of
all ages. Small crown 8vo. Cloth,
limp, 2*s.*

BAUR (Ferdinand), Dr. Ph.

A Philological Introduction
to Greek and Latin for Students.
Translated and adapted from the
German of. By C. KEGAN PAUL,
M.A. Oxon., and the Rev. E. D.
STONE, M.A., late Fellow of King's
College, Cambridge, and Assistant
Master at Eton. Second and re-
vised edition. Crown 8vo. Cloth,
price 6*s.*

BAYNES (Rev. Canon R. H.).

At the Communion Time.
A Manual for Holy Communion.
With a preface by the Right Rev.
the Lord Bishop of Derry and
Raphoe. Cloth, price 1*s. 6d.*
*** Can also be had bound in
French morocco, price 2*s. 6d.* ; Per-
sian morocco, price 3*s.* ; Calf, or
Turkey morocco, price 3*s. 6d.*

BAYNES (Rev. Canon R. H.).—
continued.
Home Songs for Quiet Hours. Fourth and cheaper Edition. Fcap. 8vo. Cloth, price 2s. 6d.
This may also be had handsomely bound in morocco with gilt edges.

BELLINGHAM (Henry), Barrister-at-Law.
Social Aspects of Catholicism and Protestantism in their Civil Bearing upon Nations. Translated and adapted from the French of M. le Baron de Haulleville. With a Preface by His Eminence Cardinal Manning. Second and cheaper edition. Crown 8vo. Cloth, price 3s. 6d.

BENNETT (Dr. W. C.).
Narrative Poems & Ballads. Fcap. 8vo. Sewed in Coloured Wrapper, price 1s.
Songs for Sailors. Dedicated by Special Request to H. R. H. the Duke of Edinburgh. With Steel Portrait and Illustrations. Crown 8vo. Cloth, price 3s. 6d.
An Edition in Illustrated Paper Covers, price 1s.
Songs of a Song Writer. Crown 8vo. Cloth, price 6s.

BENT (J. Theodore).
Genoa. How the Republic Rose and Fell. With 18 Illustrations. Demy 8vo. Cloth, price 18s.

BETHAM - EDWARDS (Miss M.).
Kitty. With a Frontispiece. Crown 8vo. Cloth, price 6s.

BEVINGTON (L. S.).
Key Notes. Small crown 8vo. Cloth, price 5s.
Blue Roses ; or, Helen Malinofska's Marriage. By the Author of "Véra." 2 vols. Fifth Edition. Cloth, gilt tops, 12s.
⁎⁎ Also a Cheaper Edition in 1 vol. With Frontispiece. Crown 8vo. Cloth, price 6s.

BLUME (Major W.).
The Operations of the German Armies in France, from Sedan to the end of the war of 1870-71. With Map. From the Journals of the Head-quarters Staff. Translated by the late E. M. Jones, Maj. 20th Foot, Prof. of Mil. Hist., Sandhurst. Demy 8vo. Cloth, price 9s.

BOGUSLAWSKI (Capt. A. von).
Tactical Deductions from the War of 1870-71. Translated by Colonel Sir Lumley Graham, Bart., late 18th (Royal Irish) Regiment. Third Edition, Revised and Corrected. Demy 8vo. Cloth, price 7s.

BONWICK (J.), F.R.G.S.
Egyptian Belief and Modern Thought. Large post 8vo. Cloth, price 10s. 6d.
Pyramid Facts and Fancies. Crown 8vo. Cloth, price 5s.
The Tasmanian Lily. With Frontispiece. Crown 8vo. Cloth, price 5s.
Mike Howe, the Bushranger of Van Diemen's Land. With Frontispiece. New and cheaper edition. Crown 8vo. Cloth, price 3s. 6d.

BOWEN (H. C.), M. A.
English Grammar for Beginners. Fcap. 8vo. Cloth, price 1s.
Studies in English, for the use of Modern Schools. Small crown 8vo. Cloth, price 1s. 6d.
Simple English Poems. English Literature for Junior Classes. In Four Parts. Parts I. and II., price 6d. each, now ready.

BOWRING (Sir John).
Autobiographical Recollections. With Memoir by Lewin B. Bowring. Demy 8vo. Price 14s.
Brave Men's Footsteps. By the Editor of "Men who have Risen." A Book of Example and Anecdote for Young People. With Four Illustrations by C. Doyle. Sixth Edition. Crown 8vo. Cloth, price 3s. 6d.

BRIALMONT (Col. A.).
Hasty Intrenchments. Translated by Lieut. Charles A. Empson, R. A. With Nine Plates. Demy 8vo. Cloth, price 6s.

BRIDGETT (Rev. J. E.).
History of the Holy Eucharist in Great Britain. 2 vols., demy 8vo. Cloth, price 18s.

BRODRICK (The Hon. G. C.).
Political Studies. Demy 8vo. Cloth, price 14s.

BROOKE (Rev. S. A.), M. A.
The Late Rev. F. W. Robertson, M.A., Life and Letters of. Edited by.
I. Uniform with the Sermons. 2 vols. With Steel Portrait. Price 7s. 6d.
II. Library Edition. 8vo. With Portrait. Price 12s.
III. A Popular Edition, in 1 vol. 8vo. Price 6s.

Theology in the English Poets. — COWPER, COLERIDGE, WORDSWORTH, and BURNS. Fourth and Cheaper Edition. Post 8vo. Cloth, price 5s.

Christ in Modern Life. Fourteenth and Cheaper Edition. Crown 8vo. Cloth, price 5s.

Sermons. First Series. Eleventh Edition. Crown 8vo. Cloth, price 6s.

Sermons. Second Series. Third Edition. Crown 8vo. Cloth, price 7s.

The Fight of Faith. Sermons preached on various occasions. Third Edition. Crown 8vo. Cloth, price 7s. 6d.

Frederick Denison Maurice: The Life and Work of. A Memorial Sermon. Crown 8vo. Sewed, price 1s.

BROOKE (W. G.), M. A.
The Public Worship Regulation Act. With a Classified Statement of its Provisions, Notes, and Index. Third Edition, Revised and Corrected. Crown 8vo. Cloth, price 3s. 6d.

Six Privy Council Judgments—1850-1872. Annotated by. Third Edition. Crown 8vo. Cloth, price 9s.

BROUN (J. A.).
Magnetic Observations at Trevandrum and Augustia Malley. Vol. I. 4to. Cloth, price 63s.
The Report from above, separately sewed, price 21s.

BROWN (Rev. J. Baldwin).
The Higher Life. Its Reality, Experience, and Destiny. Fifth and Cheaper Edition. Crown 8vo. Cloth, price 5s.

BROWN (Rev. J. Baldwin)—continued.
Doctrine of Annihilation in the Light of the Gospel of Love. Five Discourses. Third Edition. Crown 8vo. Cloth, price 2s. 6d.

The Christian Policy of Life. A Book for Young Men of Business. New and Cheaper Edition. Crown 8vo. Cloth, price 3s. 6d.

BROWN (J. Croumbie), LL.D.
Reboisement in France; or, Records of the Replanting of the Alps, the Cevennes, and the Pyrenees with Trees, Herbage, and Bush. Demy 8vo. Cloth, price 12s. 6d.

The Hydrology of Southern Africa. Demy 8vo. Cloth, price 10s. 6d.

BROWNE (W. R.).
The Inspiration of the New Testament. With a Preface by the Rev. J. P. NORRIS, D.D. Fcap. 8vo. Cloth, price 2s. 6d.

BRYANT (W. C.)
Poems. Red-line Edition. With 24 Illustrations and Portrait of the Author. Crown 8vo. Cloth extra, price 7s. 6d.
A Cheaper Edition, with Frontispiece. Small crown 8vo. Cloth, price 3s. 6d.

BURCKHARDT (Jacob).
The Civilization of the Period of the Renaissance in Italy. Authorized translation, by S. G. C. Middlemore. 2 vols. Demy 8vo. Cloth, price 24s.

BURTON (Mrs. Richard).
The Inner Life of Syria, Palestine, and the Holy Land. With Maps, Photographs, and Coloured Plates. 2 vols. Second Edition. Demy 8vo. Cloth, price 24s.
. Also a Cheaper Edition in one volume. Large post 8vo. Cloth, price 10s. 6d.

BURTON (Capt. Richard F.).
The Gold Mines of Midian and the Ruined Midlanite Cities. A Fortnight's Tour in North Western Arabia. With numerous Illustrations. Second Edition. Demy 8vo. Cloth, price 18s.

BURTON (Capt. Richard F.)—
continued.
The Land of Midian Re-
visited. With numerous illustrations on wood and by Chromo-
lithography. 2 vols. Demy 8vo.
Cloth, price 32s.

BUSBECQ (Ogier Ghiselin de).
His Life and Letters. By
Charles Thornton Forster, M.D.
and F. H. Blackburne Daniell, M.D.
2 vols. With Frontispieces. Demy
8vo. Cloth, price 24s.

BUTLER (Alfred J.).
Amaranth and Asphodel.
Songs from the Greek Anthology.—
I. Songs of the Love of Women.
II. Songs of the Love of Nature.
III. Songs of Death. IV. Songs of
Hereafter. Small crown 8vo. Cloth,
price 2s.

CALDERON.
Calderon's Dramas: The
Wonder-Working Magician—Life is
a Dream—The Purgatory of St.
Patrick. Translated by Denis
Florence MacCarthy. Post 8vo.
Cloth, price 10s.

CANDLER (H.).
The Groundwork of Belief.
Crown 8vo. Cloth, price 7s.

CARPENTER (W. B.), M.D.
The Principles of Mental
Physiology. With their Applica-
tions to the Training and Discipline
of the Mind, and the Study of its
Morbid Conditions. Illustrated.
Fifth Edition. 8vo. Cloth, price 12s.

CARPENTER (Dr. Philip P.).
His Life and Work. Edited
by his brother, Russell Lant Carpenter. With portrait and vignette.
Second Edition. Crown 8vo. Cloth,
price 7s. 6d.

CAVALRY OFFICER.
Notes on Cavalry Tactics,
Organization, &c. With Dia-
grams Demy 8vo. Cloth, price 12s.

CERVANTES.
The Ingenious Knight Don
Quixote de la Mancha. A New
Translation from the Originals of
1605 and 1608. By A. J. Duffield.
With Notes.

CHAPMAN (Hon. Mrs. E. W.).
A Constant Heart. A Story.
2 vols. Cloth, gilt tops, price 12s.

CHEYNE (Rev. T. K.).
The Prophecies of Isaiah.
Translated, with Critical Notes and
Dissertations by. Two vols., demy
8vo. Cloth, price 25s.

Children's Toys, and some
Elementary Lessons in General
Knowledge which they teach. Illus-
trated. Crown 8vo. Cloth, price 5s.

CLAYDEN (P. W.).
England under Lord Bea-
consfield. The Political History of
the Last Six Years, from the end of
1873 to the beginning of 1880. Second Edition. With Index, and
Continuation to March, 1880. Demy
8vo. Cloth, price 16s.

CLERY (C.), Lieut.-Col.
Minor Tactics. With 26
Maps and Plans. Fifth and Revised
Edition. Demy 8vo. Cloth, price 16s.

CLODD (Edward), F.R.A.S.
The Childhood of the
World : a Simple Account of Man
in Early Times. Sixth Edition.
Crown 8vo. Cloth, price 3s.
A Special Edition for Schools.
Price 1s.
The Childhood of Reli-
gions. Including a Simple Account
of the Birth and Growth of Myths
and Legends. Third Thousand.
Crown 8vo. Cloth, price 5s.
A Special Edition for Schools.
Price 1s. 6d.

Jesus of Nazareth. With a
brief Sketch of Jewish History to
the Time of His Birth. Small
crown 8vo. Cloth, price 6s.

COGHLAN (J. Cole), D.D.
The Modern Pharisee and
other Sermons. Edited by the
Very Rev. A. H. Dickinson, D.D.,
Dean of Chapel Royal, Dublin. New
and cheaper edition. Crown 8vo.
Cloth, price 7s. 6d.

COLERIDGE (Sara).
Pretty Lessons in Verse
for Good Children, with some
Lessons in Latin, in Easy Rhyme.
A New Edition. Illustrated. Fcap.
8vo. Cloth, price 3s. 6d.

COLERIDGE (Sara)—*continued.*

Phantasmion. A Fairy Tale. With an Introductory Preface by the Right Hon. Lord Coleridge, of Ottery St. Mary. A New Edition. Illustrated. Crown 8vo. Cloth, price 7*s.* 6*d.*

Memoir and Letters of Sara Coleridge. Edited by her Daughter. Cheap Edition. With one Portrait. Cloth, price 7*s.* 6*d.*

COLLINS (Mortimer).

The Secret of Long Life. Small crown 8vo. Cloth, price 3*s.* 6*d.*

Inn of Strange Meetings, and other Poems. Crown 8vo. Cloth, price 5*s.*

COLOMB (Colonel).

The Cardinal Archbishop. A Spanish Legend in twenty-nine Cancions. Small crown 8vo. Cloth, price 5*s.*

CONNELL (A. K.).

Discontent and Danger in India. Small crown 8vo. Cloth, price 3*s.* 6*d.*

CONWAY (Hugh).

A Life's Idylls. Small crown 8vo. Cloth, price 3*s.* 6*d.*

COOKE (Prof. J. P.)

Scientific Culture. Crown 8vo. Cloth, price 1*s.*

COOPER (H. J.).

The Art of Furnishing on Rational and Æsthetic Principles. New and Cheaper Edition. Fcap. 8vo. Cloth, price 1*s.* 6*d.*

COPPÉE (François).

L'Exilée. Done into English Verse with the sanction of the Author by I. O. L. Crown 8vo. Vellum, price 5*s.*

CORFIELD (Prof.), M.D.

Health. Crown 8vo. Cloth, price 6*s.*

CORY (William).

A Guide to Modern Eng-lish History. Part I. MDCCCXV. —MDCCCXXX. Demy 8vo. Cloth, price 9*s.*

COURTNEY (W. L.).

The Metaphysics of John Stuart Mill. Crown 8vo. Cloth, price 5*s.* 6*d.*

COWAN (Rev. William).

Poems : Chiefly Sacred, including Translations from some Ancient Latin Hymns. Fcap. 8vo. Cloth, price 5*s.*

COX (Rev. Sir G. W.), Bart.

A History of Greece from the Earliest Period to the end of the Persian War. New Edition. 2 vols. Demy 8vo. Cloth, price 36*s.*

The Mythology of the Aryan Nations. New Edition. 2 vols. Demy 8vo. Cloth, price 28*s.*

A General History of Greece from the Earliest Period to the Death of Alexander the Great, with a sketch of the subsequent History to the present time. New Edition. Crown 8vo. Cloth, price 7*s.* 6*d.*

Tales of Ancient Greece, New Edition. Small crown 8vo. Cloth, price 6*s.*

School History of Greece. With Maps. New Edition. Fcap 8vo. Cloth, price 3*s.* 6*d.*

The Great Persian War from the Histories of Herodotus. New Edition. Fcap. 8vo. Cloth, price 3*s.* 6*d.*

A Manual of Mythology in the form of Question and Answer. New Edition. Fcap. 8vo. Cloth, price 3*s.*

COX (Rev. Sir G. W.), Bart., M.A., and EUSTACE HINTON JONES.

Popular Romances of the Middle Ages. Second Edition in one volume. Crown 8vo. Cloth, price 6*s.*

COX (Rev. Samuel).

A Commentary on the Book of Job. With a Translation. Demy 8vo. Cloth, price 15*s.*

Salvator Mundi ; or, Is Christ the Saviour of all Men? Sixth Edition. Crown 8vo. Cloth, price 5*s.*

The Genesis of Evil, and other Sermons, mainly Expository. Second Edition. Crown 8vo. Cloth, price 6*s.*

CRAUFURD (A. H.).

Seeking for Light : Sermons. Crown 8vo. Cloth, price 5*s.*

CRAVEN (Mrs.).

A Year's Meditations.
Crown 8vo. Cloth, price 6s.

CRAWFURD (Oswald).

Portugal, Old and New.
With Illustrations and Maps. Demy
8vo. Cloth, price 16s.

CRESSWELL (Mrs. G.).

The King's Banner. Drama
in Four Acts. Five Illustrations.
4to. Cloth, price 10s. 6d.

CROMPTON (Henry).

Industrial Conciliation.
Fcap. 8vo. Cloth, price 2s. 6d.

CROZIER (John Beattie), M.B.

The Religion of the Future.
Crown 8vo. Cloth, price 6s.

DALTON (John Neale), M.A.,
R.N.

Sermons to Naval Cadets.
Preached on board H.M.S. "Britannia." Second Edition. Small
crown 8vo. Cloth, price 3s. 6d.

D'ANVERS (N. R.).

Parted. A Tale of Clouds
and Sunshine. With 4 Illustrations.
Extra Fcap. 8vo. Cloth, price 3s. 6d.

Little Minnie's Troubles.
An Every-day Chronicle. With Four
Illustrations by W. H. Hughes.
Fcap. Cloth, price 3s. 6d.

Pixie's Adventures; or, the
Tale of a Terrier. With 21 Illustrations. 16mo. Cloth, price 4s. 6d.

Nanny's Adventures; or,
the Tale of a Goat. With 12 Illustrations. 16mo. Cloth, price 4s. 6d.

DAVIDSON (Rev. Samuel), D.D.,
LL.D.

The New Testament, trans-
lated from the Latest Greek
Text of Tischendorf. A New and
thoroughly Revised Edition. Post
8vo. Cloth, price 10s. 6d.

Canon of the Bible : Its
Formation, History, and Fluctua-
tions. Third Edition, revised and
enlarged. Small crown 8vo. Cloth,
price 5s.

DAVIES (G. Christopher).

Rambles and Adventures
of Our School Field Club. With
Four Illustrations. Crown 8vo.
Cloth, price 5s.

DAVIES (Rev. J. L.), M.A.

Theology and Morality.
Essays on Questions of Belief and
Practice. Crown 8vo. Cloth, price
7s. 6d.

DAVIES (T. Hart.).

Catullus. Translated into
English Verse. Crown 8vo. Cloth,
price 6s.

DAWSON (George), M.A.

Prayers, with a Discourse
on Prayer. Edited by his Wife.
Fifth Edition. Crown 8vo. Price 6s.

Sermons on Disputed
Points and Special Occasions.
Edited by his Wife. Third Edition.
Crown 8vo. Cloth, price 6s.

Sermons on Daily Life and
Duty. Edited by his Wife. Second
Edition. Crown 8vo. Cloth, price 6s.

DE L'HOSTE (Col. E. P.).

The Desert Pastor, Jean
Jarousseau. Translated from the
French of Eugène Pelletan. With a
Frontispiece. New Edition. Fcap.
8vo. Cloth, price 3s. 6d.

DENNIS (J.).

English Sonnets. Collected
and Arranged. Fcap. 8vo. Cloth,
price 2s. 6d.

DE REDCLIFFE (Viscount
Stratford), P.C., K.G., G.C.B.

Why am I a Christian ?
Fifth Edition. Crown 8vo. Cloth,
price 3s.

DESPREZ (Philip S.).

Daniel and John; or, the
Apocalypse of the Old and that of
the New Testament. Demy 8vo.
Cloth, price 12s.

DE TOCQUEVILLE (A.).

Correspondence and Con-
versations of, with Nassau William Senior, from 1834 to 1859.
Edited by M. C. M. Simpson. 2
vols. Post 8vo. Cloth, price 21s.

DE VERE (Aubrey).

Legends of the Saxon Saints. Small crown 8vo. Cloth, price 6s.

Alexander the Great. A Dramatic Poem. Small crown 8vo. Cloth, price 5s.

The Infant Bridal, and other Poems. A New and Enlarged Edition. Fcap. 8vo. Cloth, price 7s. 6d.

The Legends of St. Patrick, and other Poems. Small crown 8vo. Cloth, price 5s.

St. Thomas of Canterbury. A Dramatic Poem. Large fcap. 8vo. Cloth, price 5s.

Antar and Zara : an Eastern Romance. INISFAIL, and other Poems, Meditative and Lyrical. Fcap. 8vo. Price 6s.

The Fall of Rora, the Search after Proserpine, and other Poems, Meditative and Lyrical. Fcap. 8vo. Price 6s.

DOBELL (Mrs. Horace).

Ethelstone, Eveline, and other Poems. Crown 8vo. Cloth, price 6s.

DOBSON (Austin).

Vignettes in Rhyme and Vers de Société. Third Edition. Fcap. 8vo. Cloth, price 5s.

Proverbs in Porcelain. By the Author of "Vignettes in Rhyme." Second Edition. Crown 8vo. 6s.

Dolores. A Theme with Va- riations. In three parts. Small crown 8vo. Cloth, price 5s.

Dorothy. A Country Story in Elegiac Verse. With Preface. Demy 8vo. Cloth, price 5s.

DOWDEN (Edward), LL.D.

Shakspere : a Critical Study of his Mind and Art. Fifth Edition. Large post 8vo. Cloth, price 12s.

Studies in Literature, 1789- 1877. Large post 8vo. Cloth, price 12s.

Poems. Second Edition. Fcap. 8vo. Cloth, price 5s.

DOWNTON (Rev. H.), M.A.

Hymns and Verses. Ori- ginal and Translated. Small crown 8vo. Cloth, price 3s. 6d.

DREWRY (G. O.), M.D.

The Common-Sense Management of the Stomach. Fifth Edition. Fcap. 8vo. Cloth, price 2s. 6d.

DREWRY (G. O.), M.D., and BARTLETT (H. C.), Ph.D., F.C.S.

Cup and Platter : or, Notes on Food and its Effects. New and cheaper Edition. Small 8vo. Cloth, price 1s. 6d.

DRUMMOND (Miss).

Tripps Buildings. A Study from Life, with Frontispiece. Small crown 8vo. Cloth, price 3s. 6d.

DU MONCEL (Count).

The Telephone, the Micro- phone, and the Phonograph. With 74 Illustrations. Small crown 8vo. Cloth, price 5s.

DUTT (Toru).

A Sheaf Gleaned in French Fields. New Edition, with Portrait. Demy 8vo. Cloth, price 10s. 6d.

DU VERNOIS (Col. von Verdy).

Studies in leading Troops. An authorized and accurate Translation by Lieutenant H. J. T. Hildyard, 71st Foot. Parts I. and II. Demy 8vo. Cloth, price 7s.

EDEN (Frederick).

The Nile without a Dragoman. Second Edition. Crown 8vo. Cloth, price 7s. 6d.

EDIS (Robert W.).

Decoration and Furniture of Town Houses. A series of Cantor Lectures delivered before the Society of Arts, 1880. Second Edition, amplified and enlarged, with 29 full-page Illustrations and numerous sketches. Square 8vo. Cloth, price 12s. 6d.

EDMONDS (Herbert).

Well Spent Lives : a Series of Modern Biographies. Crown 8vo. Price 5s.

A 2

Educational Code of the Prussian Nation, in its Present Form. In accordance with the Decisions of the Common Provincial Law, and with those of Recent Legislation. Crown 8vo. Cloth, price 2s. 6d.

EDWARDS (Rev. Basil).

Minor Chords; or, Songs for the Suffering: a Volume of Verse. Fcap. 8vo. Cloth, price 3s. 6d.; paper, price 2s. 6d.

ELLIOT (Lady Charlotte).

Medusa and other Poems. Crown 8vo. Cloth, price 6s.

ELLIOTT (Ebenezer), The Corn-Law Rhymer.

Poems. Edited by his Son, the Rev. Edwin Elliott, of St. John's, Antigua. 2 vols. Crown 8vo. Cloth, price 18s.

ELSDALE (Henry).

Studies in Tennyson's Idylls. Crown 8vo. Cloth, price 5s.

ELYOT (Sir Thomas).

The Boke named the Go-uernour. Edited from the First Edition of 1531 by Henry Herbert Stephen Croft, M.A., Barrister-at-Law. With Portraits of Sir Thomas and Lady Elyot, copied by permission of her Majesty from Holbein's Original Drawings at Windsor Castle. 2 vols. fcap. 4to. Cloth, price 50s.

English Odes, selected by Edmund W. Gosse. With Frontispiece by Hamo Thornycroft. Parchment, 6s.; vellum, 7s. 6d.

Epic of Hades (The). By the author of "Songs of Two Worlds." Twelfth Edition. Fcap. 8vo. Cloth, price 7s. 6d.
⁎ Also an Illustrated Edition with seventeen full-page designs in photomezzotint by George R. Chapman. 4to. Cloth, extra gilt leaves, price 25s, and a Large Paper Edition, with portrait, price 10s. 6d.

EVANS (Anne).

Poems and Music. With Memorial Preface by Ann Thackeray Ritchie. Large crown 8vo. Cloth, price 7s. 6d.

EVANS (Mark).

The Gospel of Home Life. Crown 8vo. Cloth, price 4s. 6d.

The Story of our Father's Love, told to Children. Fourth and Cheaper Edition. With Four Illustrations. Fcap. 8vo. Cloth, price 1s. 6d.

A Book of Common Prayer and Worship for Household Use, compiled exclusively from the Holy Scriptures. New and Cheaper Edition. Fcap. 8vo. Cloth, price 1s.

The King's Story Book. In three parts. Fcap. 8vo. Cloth, price 1s. 6d. each.
⁎ Parts I. and II., with eight illustrations and two Picture Maps, now ready.

EX-CIVILIAN.

Life in the Mofussil; or, Civilian Life in Lower Bengal. 2 vols. Large post 8vo. Price 14s.

FARQUHARSON (M.).

I. Elsie Dinsmore. Crown 8vo. Cloth, price 3s. 6d.

II. Elsie's Girlhood. Crown 8vo. Cloth, price 3s. 6d.

III. Elsie's Holidays at Roselands. Crown 8vo. Cloth, price 3s. 6d.

FIELD (Horace), B.A. Lond.

The Ultimate Triumph of Christianity. Small crown 8vo. Cloth, price 3s. 6d.

FINN (the late James), M.R.A.S.

Stirring Times; or, Records from Jerusalem Consular Chronicles of 1853 to 1856. Edited and Compiled by his Widow. With a Preface by the Viscountess Strangford. 2 vols. Demy 8vo. Price 30s.

Folkestone Ritual Case (The). The Argument, Proceedings Judgment, and Report, revised by the several Counsel engaged. Demy 8vo. Cloth, price 25s.

FORMBY (Rev. Henry).

Ancient Rome and its Connection with the Christian Religion : an Outline of the History of the City from its First Foundation down to the Erection of the Chair of St. Peter, A.D. 42-47. With numerous Illustrations of Ancient Monuments, Sculpture, and Coinage, and of the Antiquities of the Christian Catacombs. Royal 4to. Cloth extra, price 50s. Roxburgh, half-morocco, price 52s. 6d.

FOWLE (Rev. T. W.), M.A.

The Reconciliation of Religion and Science. Being Essays on Immortality, Inspiration, Miracles, and the Being of Christ. Demy 8vo. Cloth, price 10s. 6d.

The Divine Legation of Christ. Crown 8vo. Cloth, price 7s.

FRASER (Donald).

Exchange Tables of Sterling and Indian Rupee Currency, upon a new and extended system, embracing Values from One Farthing to One Hundred Thousand Pounds, and at Rates progressing, in Sixteenths of a Penny, from 1s. 9d. to 2s. 3d. per Rupee. Royal 8vo. Cloth, price 10s. 6d.

FRISWELL (J. Hain).

The Better Self. Essays for Home Life. Crown 8vo. Cloth, price 6s.

One of Two ; or, A Left-Handed Bride. With a Frontispiece. Crown 8vo. Cloth, price 3s. 6d.

GARDNER (J.), M.D.

Longevity : The Means of Prolonging Life after Middle Age. Fourth Edition, Revised and Enlarged. Small crown 8vo. Cloth, price 4s.

GARRETT (E.).

By Still Waters. A Story for Quiet Hours. With Seven Illustrations. Crown 8vo. Cloth, price 6s.

GEBLER (Karl Von).

Galileo Galilei and the Roman Curia, from Authentic Sources. Translated with the sanction of the Author, by Mrs. GEORGE STURGE. Demy 8vo. Cloth, price 12s.

GEDDES (James).

History of the Administration of John de Witt, Grand Pensionary of Holland. Vol. I. 1623—1654. Demy 8vo., with Portrait. Cloth, price 15s.

GEORGE (Henry).

Progress and Poverty. An Inquiry into the Cause of Industrial Depressions and of Increase of Want with Increase of Wealth. The Remedy. Post 8vo. Cloth, price 7s. 6d.

G. H. T.

Verses, mostly written in India. Crown 8vo. Cloth, price 6s.

GILBERT (Mrs.).

Autobiography and other Memorials. Edited by Josiah Gilbert. Third Edition. With Portrait and several Wood Engravings. Crown 8vo. Cloth, price 7s. 6d.

GILL (Rev. W. W.), B.A.

Myths and Songs from the South Pacific. With a Preface by F. Max Müller, M.A., Professor of Comparative Philology at Oxford. Post 8vo. Cloth, price 9s.

Ginevra and The Duke of Guise. Two Tragedies. Crown 8vo. Cloth, price 6s.

GLOVER (F.), M.A.

Exempla Latina. A First Construing Book with Short Notes, Lexicon, and an Introduction to the Analysis of Sentences. Fcap. 8vo. Cloth, price 2s.

GODWIN (William).

William Godwin : His Friends and Contemporaries. With Portraits and Facsimiles of the handwriting of Godwin and his Wife. By C. Kegan Paul. 2 vols. Demy 8vo. Cloth, price 28s.

The Genius of Christianity Unveiled. Being Essays never before published. Edited, with a Preface, by C. Kegan Paul. Crown 8vo. Cloth, price 7s. 6d.

GOETZE (Capt. A. von).

Operations of the German Engineers during the War of 1870-1871. Published by Authority, and in accordance with Official Documents. Translated from the German by Colonel G. Graham, V.C., C.B., R.E. With 6 large Maps. Demy 8vo. Cloth, price 21s.

GOLDSMID (Sir Francis Henry).
Memoir of. With Portrait.
Crown 8vo. Cloth, price 5*s.*

GOODENOUGH (Commodore J. G.), R.N., C.B., C.M.G.
Memoir of, with Extracts from his Letters and Journals. Edited by his Widow. With Steel Engraved Portrait. Square 8vo. Cloth, 5*s.*
. Also a Library Edition with Maps, Woodcuts, and Steel Engraved Portrait. Square post 8vo. Cloth, price 14*s.*

GOSSE (Edmund W.).
Studies in the Literature of Northern Europe. With a Frontispiece designed and etched by Alma Tadema. Large post 8vo. Cloth, price 12*s.*

New Poems. Crown 8vo. Cloth, price 7*s. 6d.*

GOULD (Rev. S. Baring), M.A.
Germany, Present and Past. 2 Vols. Demy 8vo. Cloth, price 21*s.*

The Vicar of Morwenstow: a Memoir of the Rev. R. S. Hawker. With Portrait. Third Edition, revised. Square post 8vo. Cloth, 10*s. 6d.*

GREENOUGH (Mrs. Richard).
Mary Magdalene : A Poem. Large post 8vo. Parchment antique, price 6*s.*

GRIFFITH (Thomas), A.M.
The Gospel of the Divine Life. A Study of the Fourth Evangelist. Demy 8vo. Cloth, price 14*s.*

GRIMLEY (Rev. H. N.), M.A.
Tremadoc Sermons, chiefly on the SPIRITUAL BODY, the UNSEEN WORLD, and the DIVINE HUMANITY. Second Edition. Crown 8vo. Cloth, price 6*s.*

GRÜNER (M. L.).
Studies of Blast Furnace Phenomena. Translated by L. D. B. Gordon, F.R.S.E., F.G.S. Demy 8vo. Cloth, price 7*s. 6d.*

GURNEY (Rev. Archer).
Words of Faith and Cheer. A Mission of Instruction and Suggestion. Crown 8vo. Cloth, price 6*s.*

Gwen : A Drama in Monologue. By the Author of the " Epic of Hades." Second Edition. Fcap. 8vo. Cloth, price 5*s.*

HAECKEL (Prof. Ernst).
The History of Creation. Translation revised by Professor E. Ray Lankester, M.A., F.R.S. With Coloured Plates and Genealogical Trees of the various groups of both plants and animals. 2 vols. Second Edition. Post 8vo. Cloth, price 32*s.*

The History of the Evolution of Man. With numerous Illustrations. 2 vols. Large post 8vo. Cloth, price 32*s.*

Freedom in Science and Teaching. From the German of Ernst Haeckel, with a Prefatory Note by T. H. Huxley, F.R.S. Crown 8vo. Cloth, price 5*s.*

HAKE (A. Egmont).
Paris Originals, with twenty etchings, by Léon Richeton. Large post 8vo. Cloth, price 14*s.*

Halleck's International Law; or, Rules Regulating the Intercourse of States in Peace and War. A New Edition, revised, with Notes and Cases. By Sir Sherston Baker, Bart. 2 vols. Demy 8vo. Cloth, price 38*s.*

HARDY (Thomas).
A Pair of Blue Eyes. New Edition. With Frontispiece. Crown 8vo. Cloth, price 6*s.*

The Return of the Native. New Edition. With Frontispiece. Crown 8vo. Cloth, price 6*s.*

HARRISON (Lieut.-Col. R.).
The Officer's Memorandum Book for Peace and War. Third Edition. Oblong 32mo. roan, with pencil, price 3*s. 6d.*

HARTINGTON (The Right Hon. the Marquis of), M.P.
Election Speeches in 1879 and 1880. With Address to the Electors of North-East Lancashire. Crown 8vo. Cloth, price 3*s. 6d.*

HAWEIS (Rev. H. R.), M.A.
Arrows in the Air. Crown 8vo. Second Edition. Cloth, price 6*s.*

HAWEIS (Rev. H. R.), M.A.—
continued.
Current Coin. Materialism—
The Devil—Crime—Drunkenness—
Pauperism—Emotion—Recreation—
The Sabbath. Third Edition. Crown
8vo. Cloth, price 6s.
Speech in Season. Fourth
Edition. Crown 8vo. Cloth, price 9s.
Thoughts for the Times.
Eleventh Edition. Crown 8vo. Cloth,
price 7s. 6d.
Unsectarian Family
Prayers. New and Cheaper Edition.
Fcap. 8vo. Cloth, price 1s. 6d.

HAWKER (Robert Stephen).
The Poetical Works of.
Now first collected and arranged
with a prefatory notice by J. G.
Godwin. With Portrait. Crown 8vo.
Cloth, price 12s.

HAWKINS (Edwards Comer-
ford).
Spirit and Form. Sermons
preached in the parish church of
Leatherhead. Crown 8vo. Cloth,
price 6s.

HAWTREY (Edward M.).
Corydalis. A Story of the
Sicilian Expedition. Small crown
8vo. Cloth, price 3s. 6d.

HAYES (A. H.).
New Colorado and the
Santa Fé Trail. With map and
60 Illustrations. Crown 8vo. Cloth,
price 9s.

HEIDENHAIN (Rudolf), M.D.
Animal Magnetism. Physiological Observations. Translated
from the Fourth German Edition,
by L. C. Wooldridge. With a Preface by G. R. Romanes, F.R.S.
Crown 8vo. Cloth, price 2s. 6d.

HELLWALD (Baron F. von).
The Russians in Central
Asia. A Critical Examination,
down to the present time, of the
Geography and History of Central
Asia. Translated by Lieut.-Col.
Theodore Wirgman, LL.B. Large
post 8vo. With Map. Cloth,
price 12s.

HELVIG (Major H.).
The Operations of the Ba-
varian Army Corps. Translated
by Captain G. S. Schwabe. With
Five large Maps. In 2 vols. Demy
8vo. Cloth, price 24s.

HELVIG (Major H.).—*continued.*
Tactical Examples: Vol. I.
The Battalion, price 15s. Vol. II. The
Regiment and Brigade, price 10s. 6d.
Translated from the German by Col.
Sir Lumley Graham. With numerous
Diagrams. Demy 8vo. Cloth.

HERFORD (Brooke).
The Story of Religion in
England. A Book for Young Folk.
Crown 8vo. Cloth, price 5s.

HINTON (James).
Life and Letters of. Edited
by Ellice Hopkins, with an Introduc-
tion by Sir W. W. Gull, Bart., and
Portrait engraved on Steel by C. H.
Jeens. Second Edition. Crown 8vo.
Cloth, 8s. 6d.
Chapters on the Art of
Thinking, and other Essays.
With an Introduction by Shadworth
Hodgson. Edited by C. H. Hinton.
Crown 8vo. Cloth, price 8s. 6d.
The Place of the Physician.
To which is added ESSAYS ON THE
LAW OF HUMAN LIFE, AND ON THE
RELATION BETWEEN ORGANIC AND
INORGANIC WORLDS. Second Edi-
tion. Crown 8vo. Cloth, price 3s. 6d.
Physiology for Practical
Use. By various Writers. With 50
Illustrations. Third and cheaper edi-
tion. Crown 8vo. Cloth, price 5s.
An Atlas of Diseases of the
Membrana Tympani. With De-
scriptive Text. Post 8vo. Price £6 6s.
The Questions of Aural
Surgery. With Illustrations. 2 vols.
Post 8vo. Cloth, price 12s. 6d.
The Mystery of Pain.
New Edition. Fcap. 8vo. Cloth
limp, 1s.

HOCKLEY (W. B.).
Tales of the Zenana; or,
A Nuwab's Leisure Hours. By the
Author of " Pandurang Hari." With
a Preface by Lord Stanley of Alder-
ley. 2 vols. Crown 8vo. Cloth,
price 21s.
Pandurang Hari; or, Me-
moirs of a Hindoo. A Tale of
Mahratta Life sixty years ago. With
a Preface by Sir H. Bartle E.
Frere, G. C. S. I., &c. New and
Cheaper Edition. Crown 8vo. Cloth,
price 6s.

HOFFBAUER (Capt.).
The German Artillery in
the Battles near Metz. Based
on the official reports of the German
Artillery. Translated by Capt. E.
O. Hollist. With Map and Plans.
Demy 8vo. Cloth, price 21s.

HOLMES (E. G. A.).
Poems. First and Second Series. Fcap. 8vo. Cloth, price 5s. each.

HOOPER (Mary).
Little Dinners: How to
Serve them with Elegance and
Economy. Thirteenth Edition.
Crown 8vo. Cloth, price 5s.

Cookery for Invalids, Per-
sons of Delicate Digestion, and
Children. Crown 8vo. Cloth, price
3s. 6d.

Every-Day Meals. Being
Economical and Wholesome Recipes
for Breakfast, Luncheon, and Supper. Second Edition. Crown 8vo.
Cloth, price 5s.

HOOPER (Mrs. G.).
The House of Raby. With
a Frontispiece. Crown 8vo. Cloth,
price 3s. 6d.

HOPKINS (Ellice).
Life and Letters of James
Hinton, with an Introduction by Sir
W. W. Gull, Bart., and Portrait en-
graved on Steel by C. H. Jeens.
Second Edition. Crown 8vo. Cloth
price 8s. 6d.

HOPKINS (M.).
The Port of Refuge; or,
Counsel and Aid to Shipmasters in
Difficulty, Doubt, or Distress. Crown
8vo. Second and Revised Edition.
Cloth, price 6s.

HORNER (The Misses).
Walks in Florence. A New
and thoroughly Revised Edition. 2
vols. Crown 8vo. Cloth limp. With
Illustrations.
Vol. I.—Churches, Streets, and
Palaces. 10s. 6d. Vol. II.—Public
Galleries and Museums. 5s.

HULL (Edmund C. P.).
The European in India.
With a MEDICAL GUIDE FOR ANGLO-
INDIANS. By R. R. S. Mair, M.D.,
F.R.C.S.E. Third Edition, Revised
and Corrected. Post 8vo. Cloth,
price 6s.

HUTCHISON (Lieut.-Col. F. J.),
and Capt. G. H. MACGREGOR.
Military Sketching and Re-
connaissance. With Fifteen Plates.
Second edition. Small 8vo. Cloth,
price 6s.
The first Volume of Military Handbooks for Regimental Officers. Edited
by Lieut.-Col. C. B. BRACKENBURY,
R.A., A.A.G.

HUTTON (Arthur), M.A.
The Anglican Ministry. Its
Nature and Value in relation to the
Catholic Priesthood. With a Pre-
face by his Eminence Cardinal New-
man. Demy 8vo. Cloth, price 14s.

INCHBOLD (J. W.).
Annus Amoris. Sonnets.
Fcap. 8vo. Cloth, price 4s. 6d.

INGELOW (Jean).
Off the Skelligs. A Novel.
With Frontispiece. Second Edition.
Crown 8vo. Cloth, price 6s.

The Little Wonder-horn.
A Second Series of "Stories Told to
a Child." With Fifteen Illustrations.
Small 8vo. Cloth, price 2s. 6d.

Indian Bishoprics. By an
Indian Churchman. Demy 8vo. 6d.

International Scientific
Series (The).
I. **Forms of Water:** A Fami-
liar Exposition of the Origin and
Phenomena of Glaciers. By J.
Tyndall, LL.D., F.R.S. With 25
Illustrations. Seventh Edition. Crown
8vo. Cloth, price 5s.
II. **Physics and Politics;** or,
Thoughts on the Application of the
Principles of "Natural Selection"
and "Inheritance" to Political So
ciety. By Walter Bagehot. Fifth
Edition. Crown 8vo. Cloth, price 4s.
III. **Foods.** By Edward Smith,
M.D., &c. With numerous Illus-
trations. Seventh Edition. Crown
8vo. Cloth, price 5s.
IV. **Mind and Body:** The Theo-
ries of their Relation. By Alexander
Bain, LL.D. With Four Illustra-
tions. Tenth Edition. Crown 8vo.
Cloth, price 4s.
V. **The Study of Sociology.**
By Herbert Spencer. Eighth Edition.
Crown 8vo. Cloth, price 5s.

International Scientific Series (The)—*continued.*

VI. On the Conservation of Energy. By Balfour Stewart, LL.D., &c. With 14 Illustrations. Fifth Edition. Crown 8vo. Cloth, price 5s.

VII. Animal Locomotion; or, Walking, Swimming, and Flying. By J. B. Pettigrew, M.D., &c. With 130 Illustrations. Second Edition. Crown 8vo. Cloth, price 5s.

VIII. Responsibility in Mental Disease. By Henry Maudsley, M.D. Third Edition. Crown 8vo. Cloth, price 5s.

IX. The New Chemistry. By Professor J. P. Cooke. With 31 Illustrations. Fifth Edition. Crown 8vo. Cloth, price 5s.

X. The Science of Law. By Prof. Sheldon Amos. Fourth Edition. Crown 8vo. Cloth, price 5s.

XI. Animal Mechanism. A Treatise on Terrestrial and Aerial Locomotion. By Prof. E. J. Marey. With 117 Illustrations. Second Edition. Crown 8vo. Cloth, price 5s.

XII. The Doctrine of Descent and Darwinism. By Prof. Osca Schmidt. With 26 Illustrations. Third Edition. Crown 8vo. Cloth, price 5s.

XIII. The History of the Conflict between Religion and Science. By J. W. Draper, M.D., LL.D. Fourteenth Edition. Crown 8vo. Cloth, price 5s.

XIV. Fungi; their Nature, Influences, Uses, &c. By M. C. Cooke, LL.D. Edited by the Rev. M. J. Berkeley, F.L.S. With numerous Illustrations. Second Edition. Crown 8vo. Cloth, price 5s.

XV. The Chemical Effects of Light and Photography. By Dr. Hermann Vogel. With 100 Illustrations. Third and Revised Edition. Crown 8vo. Cloth, price 5s.

XVI. The Life and Growth of Language. By Prof. William Dwight Whitney. Second Edition. Crown 8vo. Cloth, price 5s.

XVII. Money and the Mechanism of Exchange. By W. Stanley Jevons, F.R.S. Fourth Edition. Crown 8vo. Cloth, price 5s.

International Scientific Series (The)—*continued.*

XVIII. The Nature of Light: With a General Account of Physical Optics. By Dr. Eugene Lommel. With 188 Illustrations and a table of Spectra in Chromo-lithography. Third Edition. Crown 8vo. Cloth, price 5s.

XIX. Animal Parasites and Messmates. By M. Van Beneden. With 83 Illustrations. Second Edition. Crown 8vo. Cloth, price 5s.

XX. Fermentation. By Prof. Schützenberger. With 28 Illustrations. Third Edition. Crown 8vo. Cloth, price 5s.

XXI. The Five Senses of Man. By Prof. Bernstein. With 91 Illustrations. Second Edition. Crown 8vo. Cloth, price 5s.

XXII. The Theory of Sound in its Relation to Music. By Prof. Pietro Blaserna. With numerous Illustrations. Second Edition. Crown 8vo. Cloth, price 5s.

XXIII. Studies in Spectrum Analysis. By J. Norman Lockyer. F.R.S. With six photographic Illustrations of Spectra, and numerous engravings on wood. Crown 8vo. Second Edition. Cloth, price 6s. 6d.

XXIV. A History of the Growth of the Steam Engine. By Prof. R. H. Thurston. With numerous Illustrations. Second Edition. Crown 8vo. Cloth, price 6s. 6d.

XXV. Education as a Science. By Alexander Bain, LL.D. Third Edition. Crown 8vo. Cloth, price 5s.

XXVI. The Human Species. By Prof. A. de Quatrefages. Third Edition. Crown 8vo. Cloth, price 5s.

XXVII. Modern Chromatics. With Applications to Art and Industry, by Ogden N. Rood. Second Edition. With 130 original Illustrations. Crown 8vo. Cloth, price 5s.

XXVIII. The Crayfish: an Introduction to the Study of Zoology. By Prof. T. H. Huxley. Second edition. With eighty-two Illustrations. Crown 8vo. Cloth, price 5s.

XXIX. The Brain as an Organ of Mind. By H. Charlton Bastian, M.D. With numerous Illustrations. Second Edition. Crown 8vo. Cloth, price 5s.

International Scientific Series (The)—*continued*.

XXX. The Atomic Theory. By Prof. Ad. Wurtz. Translated by E. Clemin-Shaw. Second Edition. Crown 8vo. Cloth, price 5s.

XXXI. The Natural Conditions of Existence as they affect Animal Life. By Karl Semper. Second Edition. Crown 8vo. Cloth, price 5s.

XXXII. General Physiology of Muscles and Nerves. By Prof. J. Rosenthal. Second Edition, with illustrations. Crown 8vo. Cloth, price 5s.

XXXIII. Sight: an Exposition of the Principles of Monocular and Binocular Vision. By Joseph Le Conte, LL.D. With numerous illustrations. Crown 8vo. Cloth, price 5s.

JENKINS (Rev. Canon).
The Girdle Legend of Prato. Small crown 8vo. Cloth, price 2s.

JENKINS (E.) and RAYMOND (J.).
The Architect's Legal Handbook. Third Edition Revised. Crown 8vo. Cloth, price 6s.

JENKINS (Rev. R. C.), M.A.
The Privilege of Peter and the Claims of the Roman Church confronted with the Scriptures, the Councils, and the Testimony of the Popes themselves. Fcap. 8vo. Cloth, price 3s. 6d.

JENNINGS (Mrs. Vaughan).
Rahel: Her Life and Letters. With a Portrait from the Painting by Daffinger. Square post 8vo. Cloth, price 7s. 6d.

Jeroveam's Wife and other Poems. Fcap. 8vo. Cloth, price 3s. 6d.

JOEL (L.).
A Consul's Manual and Shipowner's and Shipmaster's Practical Guide in their Transactions Abroad. With Definitions of Nautical, Mercantile, and Legal Terms; a Glossary of Mercantile Terms in English, French, German, Italian, and Spanish. Tables of the Money, Weights, and Measures of the Principal Commercial Nations and their Equivalents in British Standards; and Forms of Consular and Notarial Acts. Demy 8vo. Cloth, price 12s.

JOHNSON (Virginia W.).
The Catskill Mountains. Illustrated by Alfred Fredericks. Cloth, price 5s.

JOHNSTONE (C. F.), M.A.
Historical Abstracts. Being Outlines of the History of some of the less-known States of Europe. Crown 8vo. Cloth, price 7s. 6d.

JONES (Lucy).
Puddings and Sweets. Being Three Hundred and Sixty-Five Receipts approved by Experience. Crown 8vo., price 2s. 6d.

JOYCE (P. W.), LL.D., &c.
Old Celtic Romances. Translated from the Gaelic by. Crown 8vo. Cloth, price 7s. 6d.

KAUFMANN (Rev. M.), B.A.
Utopias; or, Schemes of Social Improvement, from Sir Thomas More to Karl Marx. Crown 8vo. Cloth, price 5s.

Socialism: Its Nature, its Dangers, and its Remedies considered. Crown 8vo. Cloth, price 7s. 6d.

KAY (Joseph), M.A., Q.C.
Free Trade in Land. Edited by his Widow. With Preface by the Right Hon. John Bright, M. P. Sixth Edition. Crown 8vo. Cloth, price 5s.

KEMPIS (Thomas À.).
OF THE IMITATION OF CHRIST. A revised Translation, choicely printed on hand-made paper, with a Miniature Frontispiece on India paper from a design by W. B. Richmond. Limp parchment, antique, price 6s.; vellum, price 7s. 6d.

KENT (Carolo).
Carona Catholica ad Petri successoris Pedes Oblata. De Summi Pontificis Leonis XIII. Assumptione Epiggramma. In Quinquaginta Linguis. Fcap. 4to. Cloth, price 15s.

KER (David).
The Boy Slave in Bokhara. A Tale of Central Asia. With Illustrations. Crown 8vo. Cloth, price 3s. 6d.

The Wild Horseman of the Pampas. Illustrated. Crown 8vo. Cloth, price 3s. 6d.

KERNER (Dr. A.), Professor of Botany in the University of Innsbruck.
Flowers and their Unbidden Guests. Translation edited by W. OGLE, M.A., M.D., and a prefatory letter by C. Darwin, F.R.S. With Illustrations. Sq. 8vo. Cloth, price 9s.

KIDD (Joseph), M.D.
The Laws of Therapeutics, or, the Science and Art of Medicine. Second Edition. Crown 8vo. Cloth, price 6s.

KINAHAN (G. Henry), M.R.I.A., &c., of her Majesty's Geological Survey.
Manual of the Geology of Ireland. With 8 Plates, 26 Woodcuts, and a Map of Ireland, geologically coloured. Square 8vo. Cloth, price 15s.

KING (Mrs. Hamilton).
The Disciples. Fourth Edition, with Portrait and Notes. Crown 8vo. Cloth, price 7s. 6d.
Aspromonte, and other Poems. Second Edition. Fcap. 8vo. Cloth, price 4s. 6d.

KING (Edward).
Echoes from the Orient. With Miscellaneous Poems. Small crown 8vo. Cloth, price 3s. 6d.

KINGSLEY (Charles), M.A.
Letters and Memories of his Life. Edited by his WIFE. With 2 Steel engraved Portraits and numerous Illustrations on Wood, and a Facsimile of his Handwriting. Thirteenth Edition. 2 vols. Demy 8vo. Cloth, price 36s.
*** Also the ninth Cabinet Edition in 2 vols. Crown 8vo. Cloth, price 12s.
All Saints' Day and other Sermons. Second Edition. Crown 8vo. Cloth, 7s. 6d.
True Words for Brave Men: a Book for Soldiers' and Sailors' Libraries. Eighth Edition. Crown 8vo. Cloth, price 2s. 6d.

KNIGHT (Professor W.).
Studies in Philosophy and Literature. Large post 8vo. Cloth, price 7s. 6d.

KNOX (Alexander A.).
The New Playground : or, Wanderings in Algeria. Large crown 8vo. Cloth, price 10s. 6d.

LACORDAIRE (Rev. Père).
Life : Conferences delivered at Toulouse. A New and Cheaper Edition. Crown 8vo. Cloth, price 3s. 6d.

LAIRD-CLOWES (W.).
Love's Rebellion : a Poem. Fcap. 8vo. Cloth, price 3s. 6d.

LAMONT (Martha MacDonald).
The Gladiator : A Life under the Roman Empire in the beginning of the Third Century. With four Illustrations by H. M. Paget. Extra fcap. 8vo. Cloth, price 3s. 6d.

LANG (A.).
XXII Ballades in Blue China. Elzevir. 8vo. Parchment, price 3s. 6d.

LAYMANN (Capt.).
The Frontal Attack of Infantry. Translated by Colonel Edward Newdigate. Crown 8vo. Cloth, price 2s. 6d.

LEANDER (Richard).
Fantastic Stories. Translated from the German by Paulina B. Granville. With Eight full-page Illustrations by M. E. Fraser-Tytler. Crown 8vo. Cloth, price 5s.

LEE (Rev. F. G.), D.C.L.
The Other World ; or, Glimpses of the Supernatural. 2 vols. A New Edition. Crown 8vo. Cloth, price 15s.

LEE (Holme).
Her Title of Honour. A Book for Girls. New Edition. With a Frontispiece. Crown 8vo. Cloth, price 5s.

LEIGHTON (Robert).
Records and other Poems. With Portrait. Small crown 8vo. Cloth, price 7s. 6d.

LEWIS (Edward Dillon).
A Draft Code of Criminal Law and Procedure. Demy 8vo. Cloth, price 21s.

LEWIS (Mary A.).
A Rat with Three Tales. New and cheaper edition. With Four Illustrations by Catherine F. Frere. Crown 8vo. Cloth, price 3s. 6d.

LINDSAY(W. Lauder), M.D., &c.

Mind in the Lower Animals in Health and Disease. 2 vols. Demy 8vo. Cloth, price 32s.

LLOYD (Francis) and Charles Tebbitt.

Extension of Empire Weakness? Deficits Ruin? With a Practical Scheme for the Reconstruction of Asiatic Turkey. Small crown 8vo. Cloth, price 3s. 6d.

LOCKER (F.).

London Lyrics. A New and Revised Edition, with Additions and a Portrait of the Author. Crown 8vo. Cloth, elegant, price 6s.

Also, a Cheaper Edition. Fcap 8vo. Cloth, price 2s. 6d.

LOKI.

The New Werther. Small crown 8vo. Cloth, price 2s. 6d.

LONSDALE (Margaret).

Sister Dora. A Biography, with Portrait engraved on steel by C. H. Jeens, and one illustration. Twelfth edition. Crown 8vo. Cloth, price 6s.

LORIMER (Peter), D.D.

John Knox and the Church of England: His Work in her Pulpit, and his Influence upon her Liturgy, Articles, and Parties. Demy 8vo. Cloth, price 12s.

John Wiclif and his English Precursors, by Gerhard Victor Lechler. Translated from the German, with additional Notes. 2 vols. Demy 8vo. Cloth, price 21s.

Love's Gamut and other Poems. Small crown 8vo. Cloth, price 3s. 6d.

Love Sonnets of Proteus. With frontispiece by the Author. Elzevir 8vo. Cloth, price 5s.

LOWNDES (Henry).

Poems and Translations. Crown 8vo. Cloth, price 6s.

LUMSDEN (Lieut.-Col. H. W.).

Beowulf. An Old English Poem. Translated into modern rhymes. Small crown 8vo. Cloth, price 5s.

MAC CLINTOCK (L.).

Sir Spangle and the Dingy Hen. Illustrated. Square crown 8vo., price 2s. 6d.

MACDONALD (G.).

Malcolm. With Portrait of the Author engraved on Steel. Fourth Edition. Crown 8vo. Price 6s.

The Marquis of Lossie. Second Edition. Crown 8vo. Cloth, price 6s.

St. George and St. Michael. Second Edition. Crown 8vo. Cloth, 6s.

MACKENNA (S. J.).

Plucky Fellows. A Book for Boys. With Six Illustrations. Fourth Edition. Crown 8vo. Cloth, price 3s. 6d.

At School with an Old Dragoon. With Six Illustrations. Second Edition. Crown 8vo. Cloth, price 5s.

MACLACHLAN (Mrs.).

Notes and Extracts on Everlasting Punishment and Eternal Life, according to Literal Interpretation. Small crown 8vo. Cloth, price 3s. 6d.

MACLEAN (Charles Donald).

Latin and Greek Verse Translations. Small crown 8vo. Cloth, price 2s.

MACNAUGHT (Rev. John).

Cœna Domini: An Essay on the Lord's Supper, its Primitive Institution, Apostolic Uses, and Subsequent History. Demy 8vo. Cloth, price 14s.

MAGNUS (Mrs.).

About the Jews since Bible Times. From the Babylonian exile till the English Exodus. Small crown 8vo. Cloth, price 5s.

MAGNUSSON (Eirikr), M.A., and PALMER(E.H.), M.A.

Johan Ludvig Runeberg's Lyrical Songs, Idylls and Epigrams. Fcap. 8vo. Cloth, price 5s.

MAIR (R. S.), M.D., F.R.C.S.E.

The Medical Guide for Anglo-Indians. Being a Compendium of Advice to Europeans in India, relating to the Preservation and Regulation of Health. With a Supplement on the Management of Children in India. Second Edition. Crown 8vo. Limp cloth, price 3*s*. 6*d*.

MALDEN (H. E. and E. E.)

Princes and Princesses. Illustrated. Small crown 8vo. Cloth, price 2*s*. 6*d*.

MANNING (His Eminence Cardinal).

The True Story of the Vatican Council. Crown 8vo. Cloth, price 5*s*.

Marie Antoinette: a Drama. Small crown 8vo. Cloth, price 5*s*.

MARKHAM (Capt. Albert Hastings), R.N.

The Great Frozen Sea. A Personal Narrative of the Voyage of the "Alert" during the Arctic Expedition of 1875-6. With six full-page Illustrations, two Maps, and twenty-seven Woodcuts. Fourth and cheaper edition. Crown 8vo. Cloth, price 6*s*.

A Polar Reconnaissance: being the Voyage of the "Isbjorn" to Novaya Zemlya in 1879. With 10 Illustrations. Demy 8vo. Cloth, price 16*s*.

Master Bobby: a Tale. By the Author of "Christina North." With Illustrations by E. H. BELL. Extra fcap. 8vo. Cloth, price 3*s*.6*d*.

MASTERMAN (J.).

Half-a-dozen Daughters. With a Frontispiece. Crown 8vo. Cloth, price 3*s*. 6*d*.

McGRATH (Terence).

Pictures from Ireland. New and cheaper edition. Crown 8vo. Cloth, price 2*s*.

MEREDITH (George).

The Egoist. A Comedy in Narrative. 3 vols. Crown 8vo. Cloth.

*** Also a Cheaper Edition, with Frontispiece. Crown 8vo. Cloth, price 6*s*.

MEREDITH (George)—*continued.*

The Ordeal of Richard Fe-verel. A History of Father and Son. In one vol. with Frontispiece. Crown 8vo. Cloth, price 6*s*.

MERRITT (Henry).

Art - Criticism and Ro-mance. With Recollections, and Twenty-three Illustrations in *eau-forte*, by Anna Lea Merritt. Two vols. Large post 8vo. Cloth, 25*s*.

MIDDLETON (The Lady).

Ballads. Square 16mo. Cloth, price 3*s*. 6*d*.

MILLER (Edward).

The History and Doctrines of Irvingism; or, the so-called Catholic and Apostolic Church. 2 vols. Large post 8vo. Cloth, price 25*s*.

The Church in Relation to the State. Crown 8vo. Cloth, price 7*s*. 6*d*.

MILNE (James).

Tables of Exchange for the Conversion of Sterling Money into Indian and Ceylon Currency, at Rates from 1*s*. 8*d*. to 2*s*. 3*d*. per Rupee. Second Edition. Demy 8vo. Cloth, price £2 2*s*.

MINCHIN (J. G.).

Bulgaria since the War. Notes of a Tour in the Autumn of 1879. Small crown 8vo. Cloth, price 3*s*. 6*d*.

MOCKLER (E.).

A Grammar of the Baloo-chee Language, as it is spoken in Makran (Ancient Gedrosia), in the Persia-Arabic and Roman characters. Fcap. 8vo. Cloth, price 5*s*.

MOFFAT (Robert Scott).

The Economy of Consump-tion; an Omitted Chapter in Political Economy, with special reference to the Questions of Commercial Crises and the Policy of Trades Unions; and with Reviews of the Theories of Adam Smith, Ricardo, J. S. Mill, Fawcett, &c. Demy 8vo. Cloth, price 18*s*.

MOFFAT (Robert Scott)—*continued.*

The Principles of a Time Policy: being an Exposition of a Method of Settling Disputes between Employers and Employed in regard to Time and Wages, by a simple Process of Mercantile Barter, without recourse to Strikes or Locks-out. Reprinted from "The Economy of Consumption," with a Preface and Appendix containing Observations on some Reviews of that book, and a Re-criticism of the Theories of Ricardo and J. S. Mill on Rent, Value, and Cost of Production. Demy 8vo. Cloth, price 3s. 6d.

MOLTKE (Field-Marshal Von).
Letters from Russia. Translated by Robina Napier. Crown 8vo. Cloth, price 6s.

Notes of Travel. Being Extracts from the Journals of. Crown 8vo. Cloth, price 6s.

Monmouth: A Drama, of which the Outline is Historical. Dedicated by permission to Mr. Henry Irving. Small crown 8vo. Cloth, price 5s.

MOORE (Mrs. Bloomfield).
Gondaline's Lesson. The Warden's Tale, Stories for Children, and other Poems. Crown 8vo. Cloth, price 5s.

MORELL (J. R.).
Euclid Simplified in Method and Language. Being a Manual of Geometry. Compiled from the most important French Works, approved by the University of Paris and the Minister of Public Instruction. Fcap. 8vo. Cloth, price 2s. 6d.

MORICE (Rev. F. D.), M.A.
The Olympian and Pythian Odes of Pindar. A New Translation in English Verse. Crown 8vo. Cloth, price 7s. 6d.

MORSE (E. S.), Ph.D.
First Book of Zoology. With numerous Illustrations. New and cheaper edition. Crown 8vo. Cloth, price 2s. 6d.

MORSHEAD (E. D. A.)
The Agamemnon of Æs-chylus. Translated into English verse. With an Introductory Essay. Crown 8vo. Cloth, price 5s.

MORTERRA (Felix).
The Legend of Allandale, and other Poems. Small crown 8vo. Cloth, price 6s.

My Old Portfolio. A Volume of Poems. Crown 8vo. Cloth, price 4s. 6d.

NAAKE (J. T.).
Slavonic Fairy Tales. From Russian, Servian, Polish, and Bohemian Sources. With Four Illustrations. Crown 8vo. Cloth, price 5s.

NEWMAN (J. H.), D.D.
Characteristics from the Writings of. Being Selections from his various Works. Arranged with the Author's personal approval. Third Edition. With Portrait. Crown 8vo. Cloth, price 6s.
** A Portrait of the Rev. Dr. J. H. Newman, mounted for framing, can be had, price 2s. 6d.

NICHOLAS (Thomas), Ph.D., F.G.S.
The Pedigree of the English People: an Argument, Historical and Scientific, on the Formation and Growth of the Nation, tracing Race-admixture in Britain from the earliest times, with especial reference to the incorporation of the Celtic Aborigines. Fifth Edition. Demy 8vo. Cloth, price 16s.

NICHOLSON (Edward Byron).
The Christ Child, and other Poems. Crown 8vo. Cloth, price 4s. 6d.

The Rights of an Animal. Crown 8vo. Cloth, price 3s. 6d.

The Gospel according to the Hebrews. Its Fragments translated and annotated, with a critical Analysis of the External and Internal Evidence relating to it. Demy 8vo. Cloth, price 9s. 6d.

NICOLS (Arthur), F.G.S., F.R.G.S.
Chapters from the Physical History of the Earth. An Introduction to Geology and Palæontology, with numerous illustrations. Crown 8vo. Cloth, price 5s.

NOAKE (Major R. Compton).

The Bivouac ; or, Martial
Lyrist, with an Appendix—Advice to the Soldier. Fcap. 8vo. Price 5*s.* 6*d.*

NOEL (The Hon. Roden).

A Little Child's Monument.
Small crown 8vo. Cloth, price 3*s.* 6*d.*

NORMAN PEOPLE (The).

The Norman People, and
their Existing Descendants in the British Dominions and the United States of America. Demy 8vo. Cloth, price 21*s.*

NORRIS (Rev. Alfred).

The Inner and Outer Life
Poems. Fcap. 8vo. Cloth, price 6*s.*

Notes on Cavalry Tactics,
Organization, &c. By a Cavalry Officer. With Diagrams. Demy 8vo. Cloth, price 12*s.*

Nuces : Exercises on the
Syntax of the Public School Latin Primer. New Edition in Three Parts. Crown 8vo. Each 1*s.*

** The Three Parts can also be had bound together in cloth, price 3*s.*

O'BRIEN (Charlotte G.).

Light and Shade. 2 vols.
Crown 8vo. Cloth, gilt tops, price 12*s.*

Ode of Life (The).
Third Edition. Fcap. 8vo. Cloth, price 5*s.*

O'HAGAN (John).

The Song of Roland. Trans-
lated into English Verse. Large post 8vo. Parchment antique, price 10*s.* 6*d.*

O'MEARA (Kathleen).

Frederic Ozanam, Professor
of the Sorbonne; His Life and Works. Second Edition. Crown 8vo. Cloth, price 7*s.* 6*d.*

Our Public Schools. Eton,
Harrow, Winchester, Rugby, Westminster, Marlborough, The Charterhouse. Crown 8vo. Cloth, price 6*s.*

OWEN (F. M.).

John Keats. A Study.
Crown 8vo. Cloth, price 6*s.*

OWEN (Rev. Robert), B.D.

Sanctorale Catholicum ; or
Book of Saints. With Notes, Critical, Exegetical, and Historical. Demy 8vo. Cloth, price 18*s.*

An Essay on the Commu-
nion of Saints. Including an Examination of the "Cultus Sanctorum." Price 2*s.*

Palace and Prison and Fair
Geraldine. Two Tragedies, by the Author of "Ginevra" and the "Duke of Guise." Crown 8vo. Cloth, 6*s.*

PALGRAVE (W. Gifford).

Hermann Agha ; An Eastern
Narrative. Third and Cheaper Edition. Crown 8vo. Cloth, price 6*s.*

PALMER (Charles Walter).

The Weed : a Poem. Small
crown 8vo. Cloth, price 3*s.*

PANDURANG HARI ;

Or, Memoirs of a Hindoo.
With an Introductory Preface by Sir H. Bartle E. Frere, G.C.S.I., C.B. Crown 8vo. Price 6*s.*

PARKER (Joseph), D.D.

The Paraclete : An Essay
on the Personality and Ministry of the Holy Ghost, with some reference to current discussions. Second Edition. Demy 8vo. Cloth, price 12*s.*

PARR (Capt. H. Hallam).

A Sketch of the Kafir and
Zulu Wars: Guadana to Isandhlwana, with Maps. Small crown 8vo. Cloth, price 5*s.*

The Dress, Horses, and
Equipment of Infantry and Staff Officers. Crown 8vo. Cloth, price 1*s.*

PARSLOE (Joseph).

Our Railways : Sketches,
Historical and Descriptive. With Practical Information as to Fares, Rates, &c., and a Chapter on Railway Reform. Crown 8vo. Cloth, price 6*s.*

PATTISON (Mrs. Mark).

The Renaissance of Art in
France. With Nineteen Steel Engravings. 2 vols. Demy 8vo. Cloth, price 32*s.*

PAUL (C. Kegan).

Mary Wollstonecraft.
Letters to Imlay. With Prefatory Memoir by, and Two Portraits in *eau forte*, by Anna Lea Merritt. Crown 8vo. Cloth, price 6s.

Goethe's Faust. A New
Translation in Rime. Crown 8vo. Cloth, price 6s.

William Godwin: His
Friends and Contemporaries. With Portraits and Facsimiles of the Handwriting of Godwin and his Wife. 2 vols. Square post 8vo. Cloth, price 28s.

The Genius of Christianity
Unveiled. Being Essays by William Godwin never before published. Edited, with a Preface, by C. Kegan Paul. Crown 8vo. Cloth, price 7s. 6d.

PAUL (Margaret Agnes).

Gentle and Simple: A Story.
2 vols. Crown 8vo. Cloth, gilt tops, price 12s.

*** Also a Cheaper Edition in one vol. with Frontispiece. Crown 8vo. Cloth, price 6s.

PAYNE (John).

Songs of Life and Death.
Crown 8vo. Cloth, price 5s.

PAYNE (Prof. J. F.).

Lectures on Education.
Price 6d.
II. Fröbel and the Kindergarten system. Second Edition.

A Visit to German Schools:
Elementary Schools in Germany. Notes of a Professional Tour to inspect some of the Kindergartens, Primary Schools, Public Girls' Schools, and Schools for Technical Instruction in Hamburgh, Berlin, Dresden, Weimar, Gotha, Eisenach, in the autumn of 1874. With Critical Discussions of the General Principles and Practice of Kindergartens and other Schemes of Elementary Education. Crown 8vo. Cloth, price 4s. 6d.

PELLETAN (E.).

The Desert Pastor, Jean
Jarousseau. Translated from the French. By Colonel E. P. De L'Hoste. With a Frontispiece. New Edition. Fcap. 8vo. Cloth, price 3s. 6d.

PENNELL (H. Cholmondeley).

Pegasus Resaddled. By
the Author of "Puck on Pegasus," &c. &c. With Ten Full-page Illustrations by George Du Maurier. Second Edition. Fcap. 4to. Cloth elegant, price 12s. 6d.

PENRICE (Maj. J.), B.A.

A Dictionary and Glossary
of the Ko-ran. With copious Grammatical References and Explanations of the Text. 4to. Cloth, price 21s.

PESCHEL (Dr. Oscar).

The Races of Man and
their Geographical Distribution. Large crown 8vo. Cloth, price 9s.

PFEIFFER (Emily).

Quarterman's Grace, and
other Poems. Crown 8vo. Cloth, price 5s.

Glan Alarch: His Silence
and Song. A Poem. Second Edition. Crown 8vo. price 6s.

Gerard's Monument, and
other Poems. Second Edition. Crown 8vo. Cloth, price 6s.

Poems. Second Edition.
Crown 8vo. Cloth, price 6s.

Sonnets and Songs. New
Edition. 16mo, handsomely printed and bound in cloth, gilt edges, price 5s.

PINCHES (Thomas), M.A.

Samuel Wilberforce: Faith
—Service—Recompense. Three Sermons. With a Portrait of Bishop Wilberforce (after a Photograph by Charles Watkins). Crown 8vo. Cloth, price 4s. 6d.

PLAYFAIR (Lieut.-Col.), Her Britannic Majesty's Consul-General in Algiers.

Travels in the Footsteps of
Bruce in Algeria and Tunis. Illustrated by facsimiles of Bruce's original Drawings, Photographs, Maps, &c. Royal 4to. Cloth, bevelled boards, gilt leaves, price £3 3s.

POLLOCK (Frederick).

Spinoza. His Life and Philosophy. Demy 8vo. Cloth, price 16s.

POLLOCK (W. H.).
Lectures on French Poets.
Delivered at the Royal Institution.
Small crown 8vo. Cloth, price 5s.

POOR (Laura E.).
Sanskrit and its kindred
Literatures. Studies in Compara-
tive Mythology. Small crown 8vo.
Cloth, price 5s.

POUSHKIN (A. S.).
Russian   Romance.
Translated from the Tales of Belkin,
&c. By Mrs. J. Buchan Telfer (*née*
Mouravieff). Crown 8vo. Cloth,
price 3s. 6d.

PRESBYTER.
Unfoldings of Christian
Hope. An Essay showing that the
Doctrine contained in the Damna-
tory Clauses of the Creed commonly
called Athanasian is unscriptural.
Small crown 8vo. Cloth, price 4s. 6d.

PRICE (Prof. Bonamy).
Currency and Banking.
Crown 8vo. Cloth, price 6s.

Chapters on Practical Political Economy. Being the Substance of Lectures delivered before
the University of Oxford. Large
post 8vo. Cloth, price 12s.

Proteus and Amadeus. A
Correspondence. Edited by Aubrey
De Vere. Crown 8vo. Cloth, price 5s.

PUBLIC SCHOOLBOY.
The Volunteer, the Militia-
man, and the Regular Soldier.
Crown 8vo. Cloth, price 5s.

PULPIT COMMENTARY (The).
Edited by the Rev. J. S. EXELL and
the Rev. Canon H. D. M. SPENCE.

Ezra, Nehemiah, and
Esther. By Rev. Canon G. Rawlin-
son, M.A.; with Homilies by Rev.
Prof. J. R. Thomson, M.A., Rev.
Prof. R. A. Redford, LL.B., M.A.,
Rev. W. S. Lewis, M.A., Rev. J. A.
Macdonald, Rev. A. Mackennal,
B.A., Rev. W. Clarkson, B.A., Rev.
F. Hastings, Rev. W. Dinwiddie,
LL.B., Rev. Prof. Rowlands, B.A.,
Rev. G. Wood, B.A., Rev. Prof. P.
C. Barker, LL.B., M.A, and Rev.
J. S. Exell. Third Edition. Price
12s. 6d.

PULPIT COMMENTARY (The)
—*continued.*

1 Samuel. By the Very Rev.
R. P. Smith, D.D. With Homilies
by the Rev. Donald Fraser, D.D.,
Rev. Prof. Chapman, and Rev. B.
Dale. Third Edition. Price 15s.

Genesis. By Rev. T. White-
law, M.A.; with Homilies by the
Very Rev. J. F. Montgomery, D.D.,
Rev. Prof. R. A. Redford, M.A.,
LL.B., Rev. F. Hastings, Rev. W.
Roberts, M.A. An Introduction to
the Study of the Old Testament by
the Rev. Canon Farrar, D.D.,
F.R.S. ; and Introductions to the
Pentateuch by the Right Rev. H.
Cotterill, D.D., and Rev. T. White-
law, M.A. Third Edition. Price
15s.

Judges and Ruth. By Right
Rev. Lord A. C. Hervey, D.D., and
Rev. J. Morrison, D.D. With Ho-
milies by Rev. A. F. Muir, M.A. ;
Rev. W. F. Adeney, M.A.; Rev.
W. M. Statham ; and Rev. Prof. J.
R. Thomson, M.A. Second Edition.
Super royal 8vo. Cloth, price 15s.

Joshua. By the Rev J. J.
Lias, M.A. With Homilies by the
Rev. S. R. Aldridge, LL.B., Rev.
R. Glover, Rev. E. de Pressensé,
D.D., Rev. J. Waite, Rev. F. W.
Adeney, and an Introduction by the
Rev. A. Plummer, M.A. Second
Edition. Price 12s. 6d.

Punjaub (The) and North
Western Frontier of India. By an
old Punjaubee. Crown 8vo. Cloth,
price 5s.

Rabbi Jeshua. An Eastern
Story. Crown 8vo. Cloth, price
3s. 6d.

RAVENSHAW (John Henry),
B.C.S.
Gaur: Its Ruins and In-
scriptions. Edited with consider-
able additions and alterations by his
Widow. With forty-four photographic illustrations and twenty-five
fac-similes of Inscriptions. Super
royal 4to. Cloth, price 3£ 13s. 6d.

READ (Carveth).
On the Theory of Logic :
An Essay. Crown 8vo. Cloth,
price 6s.

Realities of the Future Life.
Small crown 8vo. Cloth, price
1*s*. 6*d*.

REANEY (Mrs. G. S.).
Blessing and Blessed; a
Sketch of Girl Life. New and
cheaper Edition. With a frontis-
piece. Crown 8vo. Cloth, price 3*s*. 6*d*.
Waking and Working; or,
from Girlhood to Womanhood.
New and cheaper edition. With a
Frontispiece. Crown 8vo. Cloth,
price 3*s*. 6*d*.
Rose Guerney's Discovery.
A Book for Girls, dedicated to their
Mothers. Crown 8vo. Cloth, price
3*s*. 6*d*.
English Girls: their Place
and Power. With a Preface by
R. W. Dale, M.A., of Birmingham.
Third Edition. Fcap. 8vo. Cloth,
price 2*s*. 6*d*.
Just Anyone, and other
Stories. Three Illustrations. Royal
16mo. Cloth, price 1*s*. 6*d*.
Sunshine Jenny and other
Stories. Three Illustrations. Royal
16mo. Cloth, price 1*s*. 6*d*.
Sunbeam Willie, and other
Stories. Three Illustrations. Royal
16mo. Cloth, price 1*s*. 6*d*.

RENDALL (J. M.).
Concise Handbook of the
Island of Madeira. With plan of
Funchal and map of the Island. Fcap.
8vo. Cloth, price 1*s*. 6*d*.

REYNOLDS (Rev. J. W.).
The Supernatural in Na-
ture. A Verification by Free Use of
Science. Second Edition, revised
and enlarged. Demy 8vo. Cloth,
price 14*s*.
Mystery of Miracles, The.
By the Author of "The Supernatural
in Nature." Crown 8vo. Cloth,
price 6*s*.

RHOADES (James).
The Georgics of Virgil.
Translated into English Verse. Small
crown 8vo. Cloth, price 5*s*.

RIBOT (Prof. Th.).
English Psychology. Se-
cond Edition. A Revised and Cor-
rected Translation from the latest
French Edition. Large post 8vo.
Cloth, price 9*s*.

RIBOT (Prof. Th.)—*continued*.
Heredity: A Psychological
Study on its Phenomena, its Laws,
its Causes, and its Consequences.
Large crown 8vo. Cloth, price 9*s*.

RINK (Chevalier Dr. Henry).
Greenland: Its People and
its Products. By the Chevalier
Dr. HENRY RINK, President of the
Greenland Board of Trade. With
sixteen Illustrations, drawn by the
Eskimo, and a Map. Edited by Dr.
ROBERT BROWN. Crown 8vo. Price
10*s*. 6*d*.

ROBERTSON (The Late Rev.
F. W.), M.A., of Brighton.
The Human Race, and
other Sermons preached at Chelten-
ham, Oxford, and Brighton. Second
Edition. Large post 8vo. Cloth,
price 7*s*. 6*d*.
Notes on Genesis. New
and cheaper Edition. Crown 8vo.,
price 3*s*. 6*d*.
Sermons. Four Series. Small
crown 8vo. Cloth, price 3*s*. 6*d*. each.
Expository Lectures on
St. Paul's Epistles to the Co-
rinthians. A New Edition. Small
crown 8vo. Cloth, price 5*s*.
Lectures and Addresses,
with other literary remains. A New
Edition. Crown 8vo. Cloth, price 5*s*.
An Analysis of Mr. Tenny-
son's "In Memoriam." (Dedi-
cated by Permission to the Poet-
Laureate.) Fcap. 8vo. Cloth, price 2*s*.
The Education of the
Human Race. Translated from
the German of Gotthold Ephraim
Lessing. Fcap. 8vo. Cloth, price
2*s*. 6*d*.
Life and Letters. Edited by
the Rev. Stopford Brooke, M.A.,
Chaplain in Ordinary to the Queen.
I. 2 vols., uniform with the Ser-
mons. With Steel Portrait. Crown
8vo. Cloth, price 7*s*. 6*d*.
II. Library Edition, in Demy 8vo.,
with Portrait. Cloth, price 12*s*.
III. A Popular Edition, in one vol.
Crown 8vo. Cloth, price 6*s*.

*The above Works can also be had
half-bound in morocco.*

*** A Portrait of the late Rev. F. W.
Robertson, mounted for framing, can
be had, price 2*s*. 6*d*.

ROBINSON (A. Mary F.).
A Handful of Honey-
suckle. Fcap. 8vo. Cloth, price
3s. 6d.

RODWELL (G. F.), F.R.A.S.,
F.C.S.
Etna: a History of the
Mountain and its Eruptions.
With Maps and Illustrations. Square
8vo. Cloth, price 9s.

ROSS (Mrs. E.), ("Nelsie Brook").
Daddy's Pet. A Sketch
from Humble Life. With Six Illustrations. Royal 16mo. Cloth, price 1s.

ROSS (Alexander), D.D.
Memoir of Alexander
Ewing, Bishop of Argyll and the
Isles. Second and Cheaper Edition.
Demy 8vo. Cloth, price 10s. 6d.

SADLER (S. W.), R.N.
The African Cruiser. A
Midshipman's Adventures on the
West Coast. With Three Illustra-
tions. Second Edition. Crown 8vo.
Cloth, price 3s. 6d.

SALTS (Rev. Alfred), LL.D.
Godparents at Confirma-
tion. With a Preface by the Bishop
of Manchester. Small crown 8vo.
Cloth, limp, price 2s.

SAMUEL (Sydney Montagu).
Jewish Life in the East.
Small crown 8vo. Cloth, price 3s. 6d.

Sappho. A Dream. By the
Author of "Palace and Prison," &c.
Crown 8vo. Cloth, price 3s. 6d.

SAUNDERS (Katherine).
Gideon's Rock, and other
Stories. Crown 8vo. Cloth, price 6s.

Joan Merryweather, and other
Stories. Crown 8vo. Cloth, price 6s.

Margaret and Elizabeth.
A Story of the Sea. Crown 8vo.
Cloth, price 6s.

SAUNDERS (John).
Israel Mort, Overman : A
Story of the Mine. Cr. 8vo. Price 6s.

Hirell. With Frontispiece.
Crown 8vo. Cloth, price 3s. 6d.

Abel Drake's Wife. With
Frontispiece. Crown 8vo. Cloth,
price 3s. 6d.

SAYCE (Rev. Archibald Henry).
Introduction to the Science
of Language. Two vols., large post
8vo. Cloth, price 25s.

SCHELL (Maj. von).
The Operations of the
First Army under Gen. von
Goeben. Translated by Col. C. H.
von Wright. Four Maps. Demy
8vo. Cloth, price 9s.

The Operations of the
First Army under Gen. von
Steinmetz. Translated by Captain
E. O. Hollist. Demy 8vo. Cloth,
price 10s. 6d.

SCHELLENDORF (Maj.-Gen.
B. von).
The Duties of the General
Staff. Translated from the German
by Lieutenant Hare. Vol. I. Demy
8vo. Cloth, 10s. 6d.

SCHERFF (Maj. W. von).
Studies in the New In-
fantry Tactics. Parts I. and II.
Translated from the German by
Colonel Lumley Graham. Demy
8vo. Cloth, price 7s. 6d.

Scientific Layman. The New
Truth and the Old Faith : are they
Incompatible? Demy 8vo. Cloth,
price 10s. 6d.

SCOONES (W. Baptiste).
Four Centuries of English
Letters. A Selection of 350 Letters
by 150 Writers from the period of the
Paston Letters to the Present Time.
Edited and arranged by. Large
crown 8vo. Cloth, price 9s.

SCOTT (Leader).
A Nook in the Apennines:
A Summer beneath the Chestnuts.
With Frontispiece, and 27 Illustra-
tions in the Text, chiefly from
Original Sketches. Crown 8vo.
Cloth, price 7s. 6d.

SCOTT (Robert H.).
Weather Charts and Storm
Warnings. Illustrated. Second Edi-
tion. Crown 8vo. Cloth, price 3s. 6d.

Seeking his Fortune, and
other Stories. With Four Illustrations. New and cheaper Edition.
Crown 8vo. Cloth, price 2s. 6d.

SENIOR (N. W.).
Alexis De Tocqueville.
Correspondence and Conversations with Nassau W. Senior, from 1833 to 1859. Edited by M. C. M. Simpson. 2 vols. Large post 8vo. Cloth, price 21s.

Sermons to Naval Cadets.
Preached on board H.M.S. "Britannia." Small crown 8vo. Cloth, price 3s. 6d.

Seven Autumn Leaves from
Fairyland. Illustrated with Nine Etchings. Square crown 8vo. Cloth, price 3s. 6d.

SHADWELL (Maj.-Gen.), C.B.
Mountain Warfare. Illus-
trated by the Campaign of 1799 in Switzerland. Being a Translation of the Swiss Narrative compiled from the Works of the Archduke Charles, Jomini, and others. Also of Notes by General H. Dufour on the Campaign of the Valtelline in 1635. With Appendix, Maps, and Introductory Remarks. Demy 8vo. Cloth, price 16s.

SHAKSPEARE (Charles).
Saint Paul at Athens :
Spiritual Christianity in Relation to some Aspects of Modern Thought. Nine Sermons preached at St. Stephen's Church, Westbourne Park. With Preface by the Rev. Canon FARRAR. Crown 8vo. Cloth, price 5s.

SHAW (Major Wilkinson).
The Elements of Modern
Tactics. Practically applied to English Formations. With Twenty-five Plates and Maps. Second and cheaper Edition. Small crown 8vo. Cloth, price 9s.

** The Second Volume of "Military Handbooks for Officers and Non-commissioned Officers." Edited by Lieut.-Col. C. B. Brackenbury, R.A., A.A.G.

SHAW (Flora L.).
Castle Blair : a Story of
Youthful Lives. 2 vols. Crown 8vo. Cloth, gilt tops, price 12s. Also, an dition in one vol. Crown 8vo. 6s.

SHELLEY (Lady).
Shelley Memorials from
Authentic Sources. With (now first printed) an Essay on Christianity by Percy Bysshe Shelley. With Portrait. Third Edition. Crown 8vo. Cloth, price 5s.

SHELLEY (Percy Bysshe).
Poems selected from. Dedi-
cated to Lady Shelley. With Preface by Richard Garnett. Printed on hand-made paper. With miniature frontispiece. Elzevir.8vo., limp parchment antique. Price 6s., vellum 7s.6d.

SHERMAN (Gen. W. T.).
Memoirs of General W.
T. Sherman, Commander of the Federal Forces in the American Civil War. By Himself. 2 vols. With Map. Demy 8vo. Cloth, price 24s. *Copyright English Edition.*

SHILLITO (Rev. Joseph).
Womanhood : its Duties,
Temptations, and Privileges. A Book for Young Women. Second Edition. Crown 8vo. Price 3s. 6d.

SHIPLEY (Rev. Orby), M.A.
Principles of the Faith in
Relation to Sin. Topics for Thought in Times of Retreat. Eleven Addresses. With an Introduction on the neglect of Dogmatic Theology in the Church of England, and a Postscript on his leaving the Church of England. Demy 8vo. Cloth, price 12s.

Church Tracts, or Studies
in Modern Problems. By various Writers. 2 vols. Crown 8vo. Cloth, price 5s. each.

Sister Augustine, Superior
of the Sisters of Charity at the St. Johannis Hospital at Bonn. Authorized Translation by Hans Tharau from the German Memorials of Amalie von Lasaulx. Second edition. Large crown 8vo. Cloth, price 7s. 6d.

SMITH (Edward), M.D., LL.B., F.R.S.
Health and Disease, as In-
fluenced by the Daily, Seasonal, and other Cyclical Changes in the Human System. A New Edition. Post 8vo. Cloth, price 7s. 6d.

Practical Dietary for
Families, Schools, and the Labouring Classes. A New Edition. Post 8vo. Cloth, price 3s. 6d.

Tubercular Consumption
in its Early and Remediable Stages. Second Edition. Crown 8vo. Cloth, price 6s.

Songs of Two Worlds. By
the Author of "The Epic of Hades."
Sixth Edition. Complete in one
Volume, with Portrait. Fcap. 8vo.
Cloth, price 7s. 6d.

Songs for Music.
By Four Friends. Square crown
8vo. Cloth, price 5s.
Containing songs by Reginald A.
Gatty, Stephen H. Gatty, Greville
J. Chester, and Juliana Ewing.

SPEDDING (James).
Reviews and Discussions,
Literary, Political, and His-
torical, not relating to Bacon.
Demy 8vo. Cloth, price 12s. 6d.

STAPFER (Paul).
Shakspeare and Classical
Antiquity : Greek and Latin Anti-
quity as presented in Shakspeare's
Plays. Translated by Emily J. Carey.
Large post 8vo. Cloth, price 12s.

STEDMAN (Edmund Clarence).
Lyrics and Idylls. With
other Poems. Crown 8vo. Cloth,
price 7s. 6d.

**STEPHENS (Archibald John),
LL.D.**
The Folkestone Ritual
Case. The Substance of the Argument delivered before the Judicial
Committee of the Privy Council. On
behalf of the Respondents. Demy
8vo. Cloth, price 6s.

STEVENS (William).
The Truce of God, and other
Poems. Small crown 8vo. Cloth,
price 3s. 6d.

STEVENSON (Robert Louis).
An Inland Voyage. With
Frontispiece by Walter Crane.
Crown 8vo. Cloth, price 7s. 6d.

Travels with a Donkey in
the Cevennes. With Frontispiece
by Walter Crane. Crown 8vo. Cloth,
price 7s. 6d.

Virginibus, Puerisque, and
other Papers. Crown 8vo. Cloth,
price 6s.

STEVENSON (Rev. W. F.).
Hymns for the Church and
Home. Selected and Edited by the
Rev. W. Fleming Stevenson.
The most complete Hymn Book
published.
The Hymn Book consists of Three
Parts :—I. For Public Worship.—
II. For Family and Private Worship.
—III. For Children.
*** Published in various forms and
prices, the latter ranging from 8d.
to 6s. Lists and full particulars
will be furnished on application to
the Publishers.

STOCKTON (Frank R.).
A Jolly Fellowship. With
20 Illustrations. Crown 8vo. Cloth,
price 5s.

**STORR (Francis), and TURNER
Hawes).**
Canterbury Chimes; or,
Chaucer Tales retold to Children.
With Illustrations from the Elles-
mere MS. Extra Fcap. 8vo. Cloth,
price 3s. 6d.

STRETTON (Hesba).
David Lloyd's Last Will.
With Four Illustrations. Royal
16mo., price 2s. 6d.

The Wonderful Life.
Thirteenth Thousand. Fcap. 8vo.
Cloth, price 2s. 6d.

Through a Needle's Eye :
a Story. 2 vols. Crown 8vo. Cloth,
gilt top, price 12s.
*** Also a Cheaper Edition in
one volume, with Frontispiece. Crown
8vo. Cloth, price 6s.

STUBBS (Lieut.-Colonel F. W.)
The Regiment of Bengal
Artillery. The History of its
Organization, Equipment, and War
Services. Compiled from Published
Works, Official Records, and various
Private Sources. With numerous
Maps and Illustrations. 2 vols.
Demy 8vo. Cloth, price 32s.

**STUMM (Lieut. Hugo), German
Military Attaché to the Khivan Expedition.**
Russia's advance East-
ward. Based on the Official Reports
of. Translated by Capt. C. E. H.
Vincent. With Map. Crown 8vo.
Cloth, price 6s.

SULLY (James), M.A.
Sensation and Intuition.
Demy 8vo. Second Edition. Cloth, price 10s. 6d.

Pessimism : a History and a Criticism. Demy 8vo. Price 14s.

Sunnyland Stories.
By the Author of "Aunt Mary's Bran Pie." Illustrated. Small 8vo. Cloth, price 3s. 6d.

Sweet Silvery Sayings of Shakespeare. Crown 8vo. Cloth gilt, price 7s. 6d.

SYME (David).
Outlines of an Industrial Science. Second Edition. Crown 8vo. Cloth, price 6s.

Tales from Ariosto. Retold for Children, by a Lady. With three illustrations. Crown 8vo. Cloth, price 4s. 6d.

TAYLOR (Algernon).
Guienne. Notes of an Autumn Tour. Crown 8vo. Cloth, price 4s. 6d.

TAYLOR (Sir H.).
Works Complete. Author's Edition, in 5 vols. Crown 8vo. Cloth, price 6s. each.
Vols. I. to III. containing the Poetical Works, Vols. IV. and V. the Prose Works.

TAYLOR (Col. Meadows), C.S.I., M.R.I.A.
A Noble Queen : a Romance of Indian History. New Edition. With Frontispiece. Crown 8vo. Cloth. Price 6s.

Seeta. New Edition with frontispiece. Crown 8vo. Cloth, price 6s.

Tippoo Sultaun: a Tale of the Mysore War. New Edition with Frontispiece. Crown 8vo. Cloth, price 6s.

Ralph Darnell. New Edition. With Frontispiece. Crown 8vo. Cloth, price 6s.

The Confessions of a Thug. New Edition. With Frontispiece. Crown 8vo. Cloth, price 6s.

Tara : a Mahratta Tale. New Edition. With Frontispiece. Crown 8vo. Cloth, price 6s.

TEBBITT (Charles) and Francis Lloyd.
Extension of Empire Weakness? Deficits Ruin? With a Practical Scheme for the Reconstruction of Asiatic Turkey. Small crown 8vo. Cloth, price 3s. 6d.

TENNYSON (Alfred).
The Imperial Library Edition. Complete in 7 vols. Demy 8vo. Cloth, price £3 13s. 6d. ; in Roxburgh binding, £4 7s. 6d.

Author's Edition. Complete in 6 Volumes. Post 8vo. Cloth gilt ; or half-morocco, Roxburgh style :—

VOL. I. Early Poems, and English Idylls. Price 6s. ; Roxburgh, 7s. 6d.

VOL. II. Locksley Hall, Lucretius, and other Poems. Price 6s. ; Roxburgh, 7s. 6d.

VOL. III. The Idylls of the King (*Complete*). Price 7s. 6d.; Roxburgh, 9s.

VOL. IV. The Princess, and Maud. Price 6s.; Roxburgh, 7s. 6d.

VOL. V. Enoch Arden, and In Memoriam. Price 6s. ; Roxburgh, 7s. 6d.

VOL. VI. Dramas. Price 7s. ; Roxburgh, 8s. 6d.

Cabinet Edition. 12 vols. Each with Frontispiece. Fcap. 8vo. Cloth, price 2s. 6d. each.
CABINET EDITION. 12 vols. Complete in handsome Ornamental Case. 32s.

Pocket Volume Edition. 13 vols. In neat case, 36s. Ditto, ditto. Extra cloth gilt, in case, 42s.

The Royal Edition. With 25 Illustrations and Portrait. Cloth extra, bevelled boards, gilt leaves. Price 21s.

The Guinea Edition. Complete in 12 vols., neatly bound and enclosed in box. Cloth, price 21s. French morocco, price 31s. 6d.

The Shilling Edition of the Poetical and Dramatic Works, in 12 vols., pocket size. Price 1s. each.

TENNYSON (Alfred)—continued.

The Crown Edition. Com-
plete in one vol., strongly bound in
cloth, price 6s. Cloth, extra gilt
leaves, price 7s. 6d. Roxburgh,
half morocco, price 8s. 6d.

*** Can also be had in a variety
of other bindings.

Original Editions :

Ballads and other Poems.
Fcap. 8vo. Cloth, price 3s. 6d.

The Lover's Tale. (Now
for the first time published.) Fcap.
8vo. Cloth, 3s. 6d.

Poems. Small 8vo. Cloth,
price 6s.

Maud, and other Poems.
Small 8vo. Cloth, price 3s. 6d.

The Princess. Small 8vo.
Cloth, price 3s. 6d.

Idylls of the King. Small
8vo. Cloth, price 5s.

Idylls of the King. Com-
plete. Small 8vo. Cloth, price 6s.

The Holy Grail, and other
Poems. Small 8vo. Cloth, price
4s. 6d.

Gareth and Lynette. Small
8vo. Cloth, price 3s.

Enoch Arden, &c. Small
8vo. Cloth, price 3s. 6d.

In Memoriam. Small 8vo.
Cloth, price 4s.

Queen Mary. A Drama.
New Edition. Crown 8vo. Cloth,
price 6s.

Harold. A Drama. Crown
8vo. Cloth, price 6s.

Selections from Tenny-
son's Works. Super royal 16mo.
Cloth, price 3s. 6d. Cloth gilt extra,
price 4s.

Songs from Tennyson's
Works. Super royal 16mo. Cloth
extra, price 3s. 6d.

Also a cheap edition. 16mo.
Cloth, price 2s. 6d.

TENNYSON (Alfred)—continued.

Idylls of the King, and
other Poems. Illustrated by Julia
Margaret Cameron. 2 vols. Folio.
Half-bound morocco, cloth sides,
price £6 6s. each.

Tennyson for the Young and
for Recitation. Specially arranged.
Fcap. 8vo. Price 1s. 6d.

Tennyson Birthday Book.
Edited by Emily Shakespear. 32mo.
Cloth limp, 2s.; cloth extra, 3s.

*** A superior edition, printed in
red and black, on antique paper,
specially prepared. Small crown 8vo.
Cloth extra, gilt leaves, price 5s.;
and in various calf and morocco
bindings.

In Memoriam. A new Edi-
tion, choicely printed on hand-
made paper, with a Miniature Portrait in eau forte by Le Rat,
after a photograph by the late Mrs.
Cameron. Bound in limp parchment,
antique, price 6s., vellum 7s. 6d.

The Princess. A Medley.
Choicely printed on hand-made
paper, with a miniature frontispiece
by H. M. Paget and a tail-piece in
outline by Gordon Browne. Limp
parchment, antique, price 6s.,
vellum, price 7s.

Songs Set to Music, by
various Composers. Edited by W.
G. Cusins. Dedicated by express
permission to Her Majesty the
Queen. Royal 4to. Cloth extra,
gilt leaves, price 21s., or in half-
morocco, price 25s.

THOMAS (Moy).
A Fight for Life. With
Frontispiece. Crown 8vo. Cloth,
price 3s. 6d.

THOMPSON (Alice C.).
Preludes. A Volume of
Poems. Illustrated by Elizabeth
Thompson (Painter of "The Roll
Call "). 8vo. Cloth, price 7s. 6d.

THOMSON (J. Turnbull).
Social Problems; or, an In-
quiry into the Law of Influences.
With Diagrams. Demy 8vo. Cloth,
price 10s. 6d.

THRING (Rev. Godfrey), B.A.
Hymns and Sacred Lyrics.
Fcap. 8vo. Cloth, price 3s. 6d.

TODHUNTER (Dr. J.)
A Study of Shelley. Crown
8vo. Cloth, price 7s.

Alcestis : A Dramatic Poem.
Extra fcap. 8vo. Cloth, price 5s.

Laurella; and other Poems.
Crown 8vo. Cloth, price 6s. 6d.

TOLINGSBY (Frere).
Elnora. An Indian Mytho-
logical Poem. Fcap. 8vo. · Cloth,
price 6s.

Translations from Dante,
Petrarch, Michael Angelo, and
Vittoria Colonna. Fcap. 8vo.
Cloth, price 7s. 6d.

TURNER (Rev. C. Tennyson).
Sonnets, Lyrics, and Trans-
lations. Crown 8vo. Cloth, price
4s. 6d.

Collected Sonnets, Old and
New. With Preface by Alfred
Tennyson; also some Marginal Notes
by S. T. Coleridge, and a Critical
Essay by James Spedding. Fcap.
8vo. Cloth, price 7s. 6d.

TWINING (Louisa).
Recollections of Work-
house Visiting and Management during twenty-five years.
Small crown 8vo. Cloth, price 3s. 6d.

VAUGHAN (H. Halford), some-
time Regius Professor of Modern
History in Oxford University.
New Readings and Ren-
derings of Shakespeare's Tragedies. 2 vols. Demy 8vo. Cloth,
price 25s.

VILLARI (Prof.).
Niccolo Machiavelli and
His Times. Translated by Linda
Villari. 2 vols. Large post 8vo.
Cloth, price 24s.

VINCENT (Capt. C. E. H.).
Elementary Military
Geography, Reconnoitring, and
Sketching. Compiled for Non-
Commissioned Officers and Soldiers
of all Arms. Square crown 8vo.
Cloth, price 2s. 6d.

VYNER (Lady Mary).
Every · day a Portion.
Adapted . from the Bible and the
Prayer Book, for the . Private Devo-
tions.of those living in Widowhood.
Collected and edited by Lady Mary
Vyner. Square crown 8vo. Cloth
extra, price 5s.

WALDSTEIN (Charles), Ph. D.
The Balance of Emotion
and Intellect: An Essay Introductory to the Study of Philosophy.
Crown 8vo. Cloth, price 6s.

WALLER (Rev. C. B.)
The Apocalypse, Reviewed
under the Light of the Doctrine of
the Unfolding Ages and the Resti-
tution of all Things. Demy 8vo.
Cloth, price 12s.

WALTERS (Sophia Lydia).
The Brook : A Poem. Small
crown 8vo. Cloth, price 3s. 6d.

A Dreamer's Sketch Book.
With Twenty-one Illustrations by
Percival Skelton, R. P. Leitch,
W. H. J. Boot, and T. R. Pritchett.
Engraved by J. D. Cooper. Fcap.
4to. Cloth, price 12s. 6d.

WARTENSLEBEN (Count H.
von).
The Operations of the
South Army in January and
February, 1871. Compiled from
the Official War Documents of the
Head-quarters of the Southern Army.
Translated by Colonel C. H. von
Wright. With Maps. Demy 8vo.
Cloth, price 6s.

The Operations of the
First Army under Gen. von
Manteuffel. Translated by Colonel
C. H. von Wright. Uniform with
the above. Demy 8vo. Cloth, price 9s.

WATERFIELD, W.
Hymns for Holy Days and
Seasons. 32mo. Cloth, price 1s. 6d.

WATSON (William).
The Prince's Quest and
other Poems. Crown 8vo. Cloth,
price 5s.

WATSON Sir Thomas), Bart., M.D
The Abolition of Zymotic Diseases, and of other similar enemies of Mankind. Small crown 8vo. Cloth, price 3s. 6d.

WAY (A.), M.A.
The Odes of Horace Literally Translated in Metre. Fcap. 8vo. Cloth, price 2s.

WEBSTER (Augusta).
Disguises. A Drama. Small crown 8vo. Cloth, price 5s.

WEDMORE (Frederick).
The Masters of Genre Painting. With sixteen illustrations. Crown 8vo. Cloth, price 7s. 6d

WELLS (Capt. John C.), R.N.
Spitzbergen—The Gateway to the Polynia; or, A Voyage to Spitzbergen. With numerous Illustrations by Whymper and others, and Map. New and Cheaper Edition. Demy 8vo. Cloth, price 6s.

Wet Days, by a Farmer. Small crown 8vo. Cloth, price 6s.

WETMORE (W. S.).
Commercial Telegraphic Code. Second Edition. Post 4to. Boards, price 42s.

WHITAKER (Florence).
Christy's Inheritance. A London Story. Illustrated. Royal 16mo. Cloth, price 1s. 6d.

WHITE (A. D.), LL.D.
Warfare of Science. With Prefatory Note by Professor Tyndall. Second Edition. Crown 8vo. Cloth, price 3s. 6d.

WHITNEY (Prof. W. D.)
Essentials of English Grammar for the Use of Schools. Crown 8vo. Cloth, price 3s. 6a.

WICKHAM (Capt. E. H., R.A.)
Influence of Firearms upon Tactics : Historical and Critical Investigations. By an OFFICER OF SUPERIOR RANK (in the German Army). Translated by Captain E. H. Wickham, R.A. Demy 8vo. Cloth, price 7s. 6d.

WICKSTEED (P. H.).
Dante: Six Sermons. Crown 8vo. Cloth, price 5s.

WILLIAMS (Rowland), D.D.
Life and Letters of, with Extracts from his Note-Books. Edited by Mrs. Rowland Williams. With a Photographic Portrait. 2 vols. Large post 8vo. Cloth, price 24s.

Stray Thoughts from the Note-Books of the Late Rowland Williams, D.D. Edited by his Widow. Crown 8vo. Cloth, price 3s. 6d.

Psalms, Litahies, Counsels and Collects for Devout Persons. Edited by his Widow. New and Popular Edition. Crown 8vo. Cloth, price 3s. 6d.

WILLIS (R.), M.D.
Servetus and Calvin : a Study of an Important Epoch in the Early History of the Reformation. 8vo. Cloth, price 16s.

William Harvey. A History of the Discovery of the Circulation of the Blood. With a Portrait of Harvey, after Faithorne. Demy 8vo. Cloth, price 14s.

WILLOUGHBY(The Hon. Mrs.).
On the North Wind—Thistledown. A Volume of Poems. Elegantly bound. Small crown 8vo. Cloth, price 7s. 6d.

WILSON (H. Schütz).
The Tower and Scaffold. A Miniature Monograph. Large fcap. 8vo. Price 1s.

Within Sound of the Sea. By the Author of "Blue Roses," "Vera," &c. Third Edition. 2 vols. Crown 8vo. Cloth, gilt tops, price 12s.

₊ Also a cheaper edition in one Vol. with frontispiece. Crown 8vo. Cloth, price 6s.

WOINOVITS (Capt. I.).
Austrian Cavalry Exercise. Translated by Captain W. S. Cooke. Crown 8vo. Cloth, price 7s.

WOLLSTONECRAFT (Mary).
Letters to Imlay. With a Preparatory Memoir by C. Kegan Paul, and two Portraits in *eau forte* by Anna Lea Merritt. Crown 8vo. Cloth, price 6s.

WOLTMANN (Dr. Alfred), and WOERMANN (Dr. Karl).
History of Painting in Antiquity and the Middle Ages. Edited by Sidney Colvin. With numerous illustrations. Medium 8vo. Cloth, price 28s.; cloth, bevelled boards, gilt leaves, price 30s.

WOOD (Major-General J. Creighton).
Doubling the Consonant. Small crown 8vo. Cloth, price 1s. 6d.

WOODS (James Chapman).
A Child of the People, and other poems. Small crown 8vo. Cloth, price 5s.

Word was made Flesh. Short Family Readings on the Epistles for each Sunday of the Christian Year. Demy 8vo. Cloth, price 10s. 6d.

WRIGHT (Rev. David), M.A.
Waiting for the Light, and other Sermons. Crown 8vo. Cloth, price 6s.

YOUMANS (Eliza A.).
An Essay on the Culture of the Observing Powers of Children, especially in connection with the Study of Botany. Edited, with Notes and a Supplement, by Joseph Payne, F.C.P., Author of "Lectures on the Science and Art of Education," &c. Crown 8vo. Cloth, price 2s. 6d.

First Book of Botany. Designed to Cultivate the Observing Powers of Children. With 300 Engravings. New and Cheaper Edition. Crown 8vo. Cloth, price 2s. 6d.

YOUMANS (Edward L.), M.D.
A Class Book of Chemistry, on the Basis of the New System. With 200 Illustrations. Crown 8vo. Cloth, price 5s.

YOUNG (William).
Gottlob, etcetera. Small crown 8vo. Cloth, price 3s. 6d.

ZIMMERN (H.).
Stories in Precious Stones. With Six Illustrations. Third Edition. Crown 8vo. Cloth, price 5s.

LONDON:—C. KEGAN PAUL & CO., 1, PATERNOSTER SQUARE.

www.ingramcontent.com/pod-product-compliance
Lightning Source LLC
Chambersburg PA
CBHW020337030726
47496CB00007B/1927